LOST

LOST

S. A. BODEEN

SQUARE FISH
FEIWEL AND FRIENDS
NEW YORK

SQUARE
FISH

An Imprint of Macmillan
175 Fifth Avenue
New York, NY 10010
mackids.com

Our books may be purchased in bulk for promotional, educational, or business use.
Please contact your local bookseller or the Macmillan Corporate and Premium
Sales Department at (800) 221-7945 ext. 5442 or by e-mail at
MacmillanSpecialMarkets@macmillan.com.

Library of Congress Cataloging-in-Publication Data Available

ISBN 978-1-250-07986-2 (paperback) ISBN 978-1-250-07286-3 (ebook)

Originally published in the United States by Feiwel and Friends
First Square Fish Edition: 2016
Book designed by Anna Booth
Square Fish logo designed by Filomena Tuosto

1 3 5 7 9 10 8 6 4 2

AR: 4.0 / LEXILE: 560L

For Aunt Connie and Uncle Bud

1

Sarah Robinson sat in the soft sand, hugging her knees and watching the sun creep farther toward sunset. The waves of the lagoon were so calm, the absolute opposite of her pounding heart and trembling hands. She took a deep breath and tried to relax. Everyone else was gathered at the camp under the monkey pod trees, but she needed a quiet moment away from their commotion, not to mention the unspoken fear.

Less than three days had passed since an unexpected and sudden typhoon had killed their skipper and wrecked the HMS *Moonflight,* marooning Sarah and the others. She figured it would have been much worse to be alone. At least she had her dad, John Robinson, a widower since her mother died when Sarah was six, and Ahab, the skipper's now-orphaned Newfoundland. She wasn't that thrilled about their other companions: Yvonna Murillo, her stepmother of barely a month, and her new stepbrothers, Marco—twelve, like her—and ten-year-old Nacho.

She sighed. Honestly, who she was with didn't matter all that much. Because this brief time on the island—the sun would soon set on their second day—had been more than enough to make it abundantly clear that there was something terrifyingly wrong with the place.

Creepy. Weird. Sinister.

There were so many other words running through her mind that would totally apply, given the things that had happened so far.

The first day, Sarah had gone for a walk with Ahab. She hadn't believed it at the time—had even wondered if her lack of sleep and the hot sun had conspired to play tricks on her—but a kangaroo with lion's claws had bounded down the beach in front of her. Certain that no one would believe her, she hadn't told anyone. But then her dad and Marco went foraging for water.

When they returned, her new stepbrother confided in Sarah, telling her that he and her dad found a small abandoned house in the forest. Inside the house, Marco saw a strange red bird that didn't seem to exist anywhere in the bird book from the boat. Marco's admission made her wonder whether her kangaroo could actually be real.

Around dinnertime that first day, an awful wail echoed around the island and went right inside Sarah's head, vibrating throughout her bones. The sound rattled everyone, and she'd been relieved when it finally stopped. As if that wasn't bad enough, after they'd gone to bed, circled up around the fire, an invasion of enormous coconut crabs forced them to scale the monkey pod trees where Sarah spent the rest of the night. Alone.

As today dawned, they made plans to avoid another night with the coconut crabs, deciding to sleep in a cave that Sarah's father had found. After lunch, they were in the midst of packing for that move when the sky had dripped red, and a bizarre orb appeared, chasing them into the cave.

As they huddled inside, Sarah added up everything and knew that something was wrong. She tried to get Marco to tell the adults about the red bird, and the other weird things he'd seen. But he refused, saying they weren't real, that he'd just made them up.

She was so mad at him for making her look stupid in front of everyone. Later, Marco tried to make Sarah understand that he had lied to the adults in order to keep his mother and brother from getting even more stressed out. But she was still not over it.

When they emerged from the cave, Sarah was relieved to find the orb gone from the sky. But then came a scream.

They hurried down to their camp, and on the beach found an unconscious girl.

And that wasn't all. Next to her was a scrawled half-finished message in the sand.

Again, at the same time as the previous day, the sinister wail started up.

Remembering the moment sent a chill up Sarah's back. She turned her head to gaze at the spot on the beach where they'd found the girl. She got to her feet, and then trudged over to the words.

BEWARE THE C

What did that mean? At first she had thought that the *C* was the start of the word *crabs,* because of the terrifying coconut crabs.

But what if it wasn't? What if there was something else on the island they had to be afraid of?

Sarah shivered, and not because she was cold.

A wave licked at the bottom edges of the letters. Another followed, slurping away more, then another and another, until the tide had swallowed the remains of the words.

The next wave covered Sarah's feet, and she stepped out of the cooling water, backing up the beach until she hit the deep, soft sand. Ahab nudged his wet nose into her hand. She picked up her flip-flops, then turned and let him lead her toward the fire and the others.

Around the fire, Marco sat cross-legged next to Nacho. The girl they'd found on the beach lay between their mother and Sarah's dad, on some of the makeshift bedding.

Ahab went right to the girl and licked her face before anyone could stop him. The girl's pale green eyes popped open. Warily, they focused on the big black dog as she sat up. The girl tried to scramble backward, but Yvonna reached out a hand and spoke softly. "You're safe here. We found you on the beach."

The girl's head swung toward the ocean. Patches of wet sand stuck to parts of her thick, long ebony braids, and her eyes darted around.

Sarah handed the girl a bottle of water.

The girl seemed to relax, just a bit. She started to speak, then stopped and took a drink first. Her voice was hoarse. "Who are y'all?"

John glanced around, as if waiting for someone else to answer. Finally, he said, "Well, I'm John and this is my daughter, Sarah." He nodded at Sarah, and then Yvonna. "This is my wife, Yvonna. And her sons, Marco and Nacho." He gestured to them as he said their names.

"And this is Ahab," said Sarah. She wondered what

the girl was thinking as she gazed at each of them in turn. Latina Yvonna and her boys, and then Sarah, obviously half Asian, and lastly her dad, with his blond hair and blue eyes. Not your average family unit. Not to mention, they all looked worse for wear, positively haggard.

Everyone had scratches on their legs and arms from the earlier race through the trees to the cave when that bloody red orb had appeared in the sky. Strands of Yvonna's dark hair had straggled out of her ponytail and the bottom of her pink flowered sundress was torn.

Other than a stain on one sleeve, Marco's red Texans shirt seemed clean enough, but one leg of his board shorts had a ragged hem where it had caught on something. Even Nacho—who seemed to value cleanliness above all else and carted a bottle of hand sanitizer everywhere—was dirty. His purple Eco-Scouts shirt sported several dark spots, and a pocket of his khaki shorts was torn. Both of the boys had bare, filthy feet. Not unlike her own.

Even her dad look disheveled. His polo shirt—usually perfectly pressed—was full of wrinkles from being slept in, with a dark smudge on the left side near his ribs. Sarah glanced down at her own tank and shorts. Other than a small rip in her shorts mid-thigh, her clothes seemed okay. She patted her hair and realized her braids had completely come out, so she removed the elastic bands. She dropped to her knees in the sand and Ahab plopped down beside her with a contented huff.

Her father continued. "Yvonna and I recently married and we are actually on our honeymoon—family style, you could say. We rented a sailboat. But then a storm hit and marooned us here."

"How long ago?" asked the girl.

Yvonna answered, "We woke up here yesterday morning."

Sarah tried to comb through her long hair with her fingers. When no one said anything, she added, "We're from California."

Nacho asked the girl, "What's your name?"

Marco elbowed him. "Leave her alone."

Nacho pushed him and Yvonna cleared her throat as she glared at the two of them.

The corners of the girl's mouth went up a tiny bit. "It's okay. My name is Cashmere Broussard. But everyone calls me Cash. I'm from Louisiana."

"I love your accent," said Sarah. She gave up on detangling her hair and stuck it in a sloppy ponytail.

Sarah's dad said, "Cash, we probably should hear how you came to be here, but right now we are running out of daylight."

Yvonna's forehead wrinkled. "Should we head back to the cave?"

Cash stiffened. "What cave?"

"It's a small one, near here." Yvonna set a hand on her arm. "It's safer at night."

Cash's shoulders relaxed. "Okay. I thought y'all meant . . ."

"What?" asked Sarah.

Cash shook her head. "Never mind."

Sarah's dad stood up and then helped Cash, still shaken, to her feet. "Do you need me to carry you?"

She shook her head. "I can walk." Cash brushed some of the sand off her feet.

Sarah noticed a few cuts. "Do you need some shoes?"

Cash asked, "Do you have some?"

Sarah nodded. "Hold on." She jogged over to her suitcase under the monkey pod trees and pulled out a pair of pink flip-flops. She carried them back to the group.

Cash slipped her feet into them. The toes hung over the end just a little. "Thanks. I've been running around barefoot ever since I got here."

Sarah wanted to ask how she ended up on the island, not to mention the warning in the sand, but decided she better wait until they were safe in the cave for the night.

John asked, "Ready?" He stayed beside Cash as they formed a line and headed into the trees.

Sarah walked with Marco at the back of the group,

Ahab close behind. She whispered, "Maybe now that she's talking, she can tell us about the message on the beach."

Marco didn't answer right away, which was enough of a pause for Sarah to brace herself for some kind of snarky retort. Ever since Marco had refused to tell the grown-ups about the bizarre red bird, she wasn't sure what to think, whether she could trust him. But when he told her that he was just trying to protect his mom and little brother, she kind of understood. And though she hoped they were past being nasty to each other, given all that had happened, she still half expected Marco to be something other than kind.

Instead, Marco simply replied, "I hope so."

A little surprised, Sarah decided to trust him. She swallowed and lowered her voice even further, so there was no chance that either Nacho or Yvonna, mere steps in front of them, would hear. "Do you think we're in danger?"

Marco turned to the side and looked straight at her, his brown eyes more serious than Sarah had ever seen them. He nodded, once. Then he faced forward again, his pace increasing.

Sarah turned to look behind them. Through two trees, she could just see the sun as it touched the water. She stopped to watch. "One, two, three . . ." As she counted, the sun sank farther into the waves, until—as she breathed out "fifteen"—it was gone.

This strange day—their second full one on the island—was nearly over.

A breeze ruffled her hair and goose bumps rose on her arms. Quickly, she turned and ran to catch up with the rest, Ahab panting at her heels.

2

At the entrance to the cave, Marco grabbed the flashlight he'd left there earlier. Inside the large, dank space, their things were as they'd left them, and everyone—including Cashmere Broussard—found a place to sit on the blankets and pillows circled in the middle.

Ahab began licking Cash's face, and she gently pushed him away. But then she seemed to reconsider, as if she felt a little bad at rejecting him. She reached out and gave his enormous head a brief rub before the dog went back to Sarah. Marco thought Cash seemed to be relaxing the more time that she spent with them. But then, she'd been so afraid when she first came to, it didn't take much to appear calmer than that.

Yvonna dug out the last of the hot dog buns, and Nacho helped her spread peanut butter and jelly on them. He held up both jars and asked Cash, "More peanut butter or more jelly?"

Cash flashed a fleeting grin, briefly revealing white teeth with a tiny gap between the front two. "Definitely more peanut butter."

Nacho set the jars down and pointed at her. "Now you're talking my language."

His mom smiled and said, "Why don't you make it for her instead of talking about it?"

"I have to clean my hands first." Nacho held up the bottle of hand sanitizer. "Anyone else?"

Cash and Sarah both nodded and reached out for some. Marco and John followed suit. Nacho helped Yvonna finish making the sandwiches, and she piled them neatly on a plate. She set it down in the middle of everyone and smiled. "Bon appétit!"

Marco grabbed a sandwich and took a bite, as they all got comfortable while they chewed. Nacho ate half his bun, then asked Cash, "How did you end up in Fiji?"

Even though Marco wanted to know the answer, he said, "Let her eat."

Cash tore off some bun and crammed it into her mouth just as she said something. Marco couldn't understand what it was, until she chewed more and swallowed. "No, it's okay. Well, except for when Sarge—that's my grandpa—was in the army, he lived his life in southern Louisiana. Three years ago, when I was nine, he won the lottery."

Marco whistled and everyone else exclaimed or gasped.

Nacho asked, "So is he a millionaire?"

"Not exactly." Cash shook her head. "It was one of those scratch-off tickets. After taxes, Sarge ended up with a little less than a hundred thousand."

"Sounds like a lot of money to me," said Nacho.

Cash smiled. "Me too. But he wanted to find somewhere beautiful and exotic to retire on the cheap, where the winnings and his pension would last him. He moved to Fiji and bought a sailboat. Sarge lives on it and does charters when he feels like it. I come every summer and stay with him."

"That's cool," said Marco. His grandparents had been way old when his mom came along, so now they lived in a retirement home in Arizona. Whenever they visited, he and Nacho had to sit and do jigsaw puzzles so they wouldn't make any noise. His father's parents lived in Mexico, and only visited once a year. He wished he had a grandpa to spend time with. "You must love it."

"Yeah," said Cash. "Until this time."

"What happened?" asked Sarah.

Cash took a sip of water. "Last Monday I was at the port in Fiji—"

"That's only a few days before we were there," blurted Nacho.

Marco elbowed him. "Shut up and let her talk."

"Marco," said his mom. "Be nice."

"I'll be nice if he shuts up and lets her talk," said Marco.

His mom gave him another look.

"Fine," he said, shoving the last of the bun in his mouth and grabbing another.

Cash continued, "I was at the port in Fiji with Sarge."

"Tell us about him," said Nacho.

Sarah frowned at him and Marco groaned. "Oh, come on."

Nacho crossed his arms. "I have a much better time picturing people if I know what they look like!"

Cash smiled. "I'll be happy to tell y'all what he looks like. He's darker than me, and shaves his head, because he thinks it looks cool. And his arms are muscular and he has a lot of ink."

"Tattoos?" asked Nacho.

Cash nodded. "He got them when he was in the army. And he likes to stay in shape." She flexed her bicep. "His muscles are huge." She shrugged. "He's like in his fifties, but doesn't look that old at all."

"What did he have on?" asked Nacho.

Marco rolled his eyes and wished Nacho would just let her get on with the story.

Cash thought for a moment. "That day he had on . . . Oh! His favorite gray army shirt and black shorts."

Marco glared at Nacho. "Can we get on with the story now?"

"Fine," said Nacho. "Go on."

Cash took a sip of water, then set the bottle down. "Well, I was below in the cabin with a can of paint, doing slight touch-ups on cabinet doors and stuff." She shook her head. "I didn't think the boat needed it, but I like to help Sarge do stuff. I heard Sarge talking to someone. I snuck up a couple of the stairs so I could peek out without anyone seeing me. There was a man—"

"What did the man look like?" asked Nacho.

"Seriously?" Marco rolled his eyes.

Yvonna said, "Boys, please."

"Well," said Cash. "He had on aviator sunglasses. They were mirrored, so I couldn't see his eyes. He was really tan and had this weird short beard." With one finger, she whirled a circle around the top of her head a couple of times. "He wore this stupid-looking white safari hat." She dropped her hand back in her lap. "And a short-sleeved blue shirt. And navy blue shorts that reached nearly to his knees." She shook her head. "And then he had on tall white socks with brown sandals."

"Gross," said Sarah.

"Totally," said Cash. She shoved the last of her bun in her mouth and wiped the crumbs off her hands.

"What did the man want?" asked John. He sounded a little impatient.

Cash looked over at him. "He wanted Sarge to take him on a sail. But Sarge said no, because he and I were supposed to go by ourselves for a couple days."

Yvonna asked, "Was he alone?"

Cash shook her head. "There was a woman." Before Nacho could ask what she looked like, Cash told him. "Her hair was short and dark and didn't even move in the breeze. Her sunglasses"—Cash made circles of both her thumbs and forefingers, then stuck them to her eyes—"were huge. I couldn't see her eyes either. And her lipstick was red, like bloodred." Cash raised her eyebrows. "It was kinda weird. She didn't even pretend to be dressed for the outdoors. Not at all. Her dress was white, and her shoes, man." Cash held her hands up, several inches apart. "The heels were like this high and see-through. And had glittery straps. And she had on a bunch of gold necklaces." Cash held out her fingers. "Her nails were long and polished the same color as her lips. And she had a diamond ring on every finger, it seemed."

Sarah asked, "Was she nice?"

Cash shook her head. "No. Neither was her dog. She had this big brown purse and this little white yappy thing stuck its head out." Cash made a face and then looked at Ahab. "I like big dogs a lot better."

Sarah patted Ahab's head and smiled. "Me too."

"Did they tell Sarge their names?" asked Marco.

Cash nodded. "Laird Fox and Bettina Blackstone."

"So what happened?" asked Marco, wanting her to get on with the story. He had finished his second sandwich and burped loudly.

His mom shot him a look, so he said, "Excuse me."

Cash blew out a breath. "When Sarge told them he wasn't interested, Fox nodded at Miss Blackstone. She reached in her purse and pulled out this stack of money." Cash held up her forefinger and thumb, several inches apart.

Nacho said, "Wow."

Marco leaned in closer. Suddenly, the story was getting interesting.

Cash said, "I wasn't close enough to see the number on the bills, but Sarge's eyes got really big. And then he started to rub his chin, which is what he always does when he's thinking hard about something."

Sarah asked, "What did you want him to do?"

Cash shrugged. "I wanted him to take it. I mean,

he's got a lot of money saved, but he always worries about it. He wants to pay for my college some day." Cash tilted her head to the left. "Plus, I've always wanted to go on a sail when he has customers."

"So what did Sarge say?" asked Marco.

Cash said, "He told them he'd take them for a week." She made a face. "And Fox smiled." She waved a hand in front of her mouth. "He had these icky, yellowed teeth."

Sarah scrunched up her nose. "Ew."

"Miss Blackstone handed part of the stack to Sarge," said Cash. "She told him he'd get the rest when they were finished."

Marco frowned. Wouldn't it make more sense to say *when we get back or when we return or when the sail is over*?

John asked, "When did you set sail?"

"Not until the next day," said Cash. "We had to buy food and clean the linens in the two berths downstairs for them."

Nacho asked, "Where do you sleep on the boat?"

"Does it really matter?" asked Marco.

"To me it does," said Nacho.

"Boys!" said Yvonna.

Cash told Nacho, "Sarge and I slept up top. When I was little, he made me a secret hiding spot near the helm." She smiled, a little wistfully. "I don't fit there like I used to, but it's still my favorite place."

Sarah asked, "What happened when they came back?"

Cash frowned. "Fox had this one small brown duffel bag with him." She shot a glance at Nacho and said, "Miss Blackstone had the dog and was dressed all fancy again, with a white sleeveless blouse, black capris, black heels."

Nacho smiled at her. "Thanks."

Cash said, "Sarge had to haul her massive suitcase on board. He asked her if she was smuggling cement."

Marco laughed.

Cash glanced at him. "She didn't think it was funny. She yelled at him to be careful with it." She bent her knees and hugged them. "Usually Sarge gave the clients a few routes to choose from. But these two couldn't decide. Fox just pointed at a spot on the chart and said, 'Let's try that one.' "

Yvonna picked up another peanut butter and jelly bun and held it out to Cash.

"Thank you." She took a bite, then started talking with her mouth still half full. "But when we got to that island it was late in the afternoon. Fox had binoculars. He just stood there, staring at the shore through them."

"Did you go on the island?" asked Sarah.

Cash shook her head and ate another bite of her sandwich. "I heard Miss Blackstone ask him 'Is this it?' "

John said, "So it sounds like they were looking for a specific island."

Cash nodded. "We didn't know it then, but yeah. Because after only a half hour, Fox told Sarge we could leave. So we sailed to another island and got there the next morning."

"Did you go ashore there?" asked Nacho.

"Nope," said Cash. "Same thing happened. Sarge was getting ticked off, I could tell. Then that night we hit a storm." She pointed at the ground. "And we ended up here, at the lagoon. Sarge anchored and went down to make breakfast."

"And you came ashore?" asked Marco.

Cash frowned. "I was trying to sleep, because it had been a rough night. Fox and Miss Blackstone came up from the cabin and stood at the stern of the boat. They didn't see me, and didn't know that I could hear them."

Cash took a drink of water. "Miss Blackstone asked Fox, 'Aren't you going to see if this is the island?' And he said that it couldn't be. His island had an old volcano, like this one. But it didn't have as many trees, and had a lot more rocks." Cash took another sip. "Miss Blackstone argued with him, saying that the trees could have grown, but Fox mentioned it had only been two years and there's no way this could be the island he was looking for."

"But how did he know?" asked Marco. He wanted to

know what Fox was up to and wished Cash would get on with it.

She said, "I don't know. But Miss Blackstone must have been mad about it, because she yelled at him, said she couldn't believe that he had no idea what island it was." Her forehead wrinkled. "But then Fox said he did know. That he could never forget the landmark, not in a million years."

"What landmark?" asked Sarah. Marco was about to ask the same thing but she beat him to it.

Cash said, "The *face rock*."

"What's a face rock?" asked Nacho.

Marco sighed. "Duh. Maybe a rock with a face on it."

Nacho stuck out his tongue at Marco and turned back to Cash. "Did he say anything else? Like how he got on the island?"

Cash nodded. "He mentioned a rough sail, all the way from Africa. And that his ship was totally wrecked and he was lucky to get off before it sunk. He got rescued by a Dutch freighter, but he didn't ask them for the coordinates. He didn't want anyone else to be able to find the place. Or his cargo."

Marco asked, "What was his cargo?"

"I don't know," said Cash. "But he told Miss Blackstone it would make her a millionaire ten times over."

"Wow," said Nacho.

Cash yawned.

Yvonna said, "Cash, you don't have to finish telling us this now. You've had a long day and need to rest."

Sarah, Nacho, and Marco all howled in protest at the same time. Yvonna held up a hand. "Five more minutes, that's it. I mean it."

Sarah leaned in. "Just tell us, quick. What happened after that? How did you end up on the island by yourself?"

Cash said, "I told Sarge what I overheard. He told them we were heading back to port, but then—" Her eyes filled with tears.

Yvonna set a hand on her leg. "Oh, sweetie, this is too much for you."

Cash shook her head. "No. I want to tell y'all what happened." She swallowed. "But when Sarge told them that, Fox pulled out a gun."

No one said anything. Marco wondered how Cash could be so calm, even while telling them what happened. He said, "You don't have to tell us anymore."

"But you can if you want to," piped up Nacho.

"Nacho, hush," said his mom.

Cash said, "I'll finish." She paused a moment to take another swig of water, then she took a deep breath. "He needed Sarge to sail the boat and take them to another island. But they didn't need me. Except for insurance."

Sarah set a hand over her mouth.

Yvonna asked, "What did they do, sweetie?"

"Sarge packed me a bag of canned goods and water while Fox held the gun on him." She frowned. "Sarge was so worried. He told me to make a fire, first thing. And he promised he'd come back for me." She sighed. "So Fox and I got in the dinghy and he started rowing me to shore. I looked back at the boat, and Miss Blackstone was holding the gun on Sarge. I knew I had to try to get away."

Marco asked, "What did you do?"

"Maybe be quiet and let her tell us," said Sarah.

He glared at her, then turned back to Cash.

"About twenty yards from shore, I tried to tip the boat." She paused. "But Fox grabbed me and shoved me over."

Yvonna gasped. "Oh no."

Cash glanced at her. "It's okay. I treaded water. But then he laughed at me. He threw the bag of food in the water and it sank before I could get it. Then he rowed back to the boat."

As Cash finished telling the family her story, tears welled up again.

Marco asked, "Do you know what the cargo was that Fox hid on the island?"

She hesitated half of a second before shaking her

head. But it was enough of a pause to make Marco wonder what—if anything—she might be keeping from them about Fox's supposed stash.

John said, "I think that's more than enough for tonight. Cash has had a long day."

Sarah blurted, "But she hasn't told us about the—"

"That's enough," said John. "There will be time in the morning."

Marco knew what Sarah was going to say: *But she hasn't told us about the message in the sand.*

And he wished John hadn't interrupted Sarah, because he wanted to know about it as much as she did.

Cash swiped a hand across her eyes and nodded. "If it's okay with you, I'd rather just tell you all now. The rest of it, I mean." She glanced around the cave. "I think I'll sleep better."

The hair rose on the back of Marco's neck, making him wonder if he really wanted to hear the rest after all.

3

Sarah handed Cash another bottle of water. Cash took a drink, cleared her throat, and told them more about her past few days.

"I crawled up on the beach. Fox got back to the sailboat. Sarge lifted anchor and began to sail out of the lagoon." Cash wiped away some tears. Her voice broke as she added, "It was so hard to watch him sail away without me."

Yvonna patted her arm.

Sarah wondered what she would do if she'd been left all alone on that island. This place creeped her out enough and she had her dad with her the whole time.

Nacho asked, "What did you do then?"

"I remembered the last thing Sarge told me. And that he'd put something in my pocket," Cash said.

"What was it?" asked Nacho.

"His magnesium fire starter. He'd taught me how to make a fire in his backyard in Louisiana. And so I made a fire. A big one to get me through the night." She sucked in her lower lip.

Marco asked, "What? Did something happen in the night?"

She nodded. "Well, in the late afternoon there was this awful howl. I can't even explain it." Goose bumps rose on her arms. "It freaks me out to even think about it."

Marco's gaze met Sarah's. She said, "I think we've heard it too."

Cash said, "It was so scary."

Marco and Sarah both nodded.

"I couldn't sleep, I was so scared." Cash shrugged. "So I sat there all night. I only moved when I had to put more wood on the fire. Finally, the sun came up and I fell asleep. It was hot when I woke up. So I walked down to the water." She smiled. "This place is so beautiful. Like a picture from a postcard."

John said, "That it is."

"But then my stomach started growling and I realized I didn't have any food. I knew there was a bag of food out there and I just had to swim out to get it." She lifted and lowered a shoulder. "But I'm not that great at diving. I was trying to talk myself into it when I heard something in the trees."

"Something scary?" asked Nacho.

Cash smiled. "No, for once it wasn't. It sounded like a *meow*. I thought it can't be. I didn't really want to go barefoot into the trees, but then I heard the sound again. And if there was a cat, I wanted to find it, so I wouldn't be alone."

Sarah understood that. She glanced down at Ahab and rubbed his head.

"But I never had a chance to find out. I got two steps into the trees and I heard this *WHOOSSSSSHHHH!* and a white net fell on me." Cash shivered.

Sarah looked at her dad. He raised his eyebrows a little, like he didn't exactly believe the girl's story. Sarah asked, "What kind of a net?"

"A weird one. I tried to stop it." Cash held her hands out, fingers spread. "But as soon as it touched my fingers, it shocked me. And then the rest of it drifted down. Wherever it touched my bare skin, it stuck right to me."

"What did you do?" asked Nacho. He was absolutely riveted by her story. But Sarah noticed that both her dad and Marco looked skeptical, like they had stopped believing what Cash was telling them. Sarah began to wonder whether this girl just liked to make up stories. True, she had ended up on the island somehow, and was stuck there like they were. But the net part of her story seemed sort of . . . farfetched.

Cash became more animated, like this was her favorite part of the story. "I tried getting loose." She thrashed her arms. "But doing that and kicking my legs only made things worse. The net began to shrink. The more I fought, the tighter it got. I tried to move my legs, but they were so close together, that I fell over. My face smashed in the ground and I got dirt in my mouth. I couldn't do anything but lie there."

She paused a moment. "The net kept getting tighter, until I couldn't breathe. And everything went black."

John clapped his hands together. "Okay, I think that's enough for today. Let's get some rest everyone."

Nacho said, "But she needs to tell us what happened. What if someone comes with nets to get *us*?"

Sarah saw her dad and Yvonna exchange a glance. Yvonna said, "Sweetie, I don't think you have to worry about that."

Cash frowned at the adults. "You don't believe me."

John and Yvonna looked at each other. She said, "It's just late and you all need to sleep. You don't need to stay awake and worry about things that won't happen."

"But they did happen!" said Cash. Her gaze darted from Sarah to Marco. "You believe me, don't you?"

Sarah shifted her eyes to Marco. He looked down at the ground.

Cash stood up. "I swear, it's true. Please, let me finish."

Nacho said, "I believe you." He asked his mom, "Can't she tell us the rest?"

Yvonna widened her eyes at John. He said, "Okay. Five more minutes. And this time we mean it."

Cash sat back down. "When I came to, the net was gone. I could move my arms and legs again."

Marco mumbled, "How convenient."

Sarah shot him a glance, but Cash must not have heard him, because she was still talking. "I was on a bed in a room like the size of my bathroom back home. The lights were really bright and the walls were white. There was one tiny window up high, and I climbed on the bed but I couldn't reach it. So I went to inspect the door."

Cash held out two fingers, about six inches apart. "There was a silver strip in the door about this high." She held her arms about a foot apart. "And this wide. I pushed at it, but it didn't even budge. And one really weird thing."

"What?" asked Nacho, who seemed to be the only one still buying her story.

"The door had no doorknob."

A chill ran up Sarah's back. She didn't believe what Cash was telling them, but that detail was creepy.

Cash said, "Then the silver strip vanished. There

was just an open empty slot, and a black tray slid through with two glasses of water and a silver dome with a handle. I grabbed the tray and tried to look through the slot." She sighed. "But just like that"—she snapped her fingers—"it closed right up. Was just a silver strip again."

Marco looked at Sarah and rolled his eyes.

Cash cleared her throat.

Nacho asked, "What was on the tray?"

"A bologna sandwich and carrot sticks. With ranch." Her forehead wrinkled. "I was worried at first, that maybe there was something in it, they were trying to poison me or something. But I was so hungry that I ate the whole thing."

Sarah tried not to laugh. Really? Captured by someone, held prisoner, and she gets served ranch with her carrots? Sarah yawned. "I think I need to go to bed."

"But I'm not done," said Cash.

"Yeah," said Nacho. "She's not done."

Yvonna said, "That's enough for tonight. Cash can finish her story tomorrow."

"Y'all *don't* believe me." Cash sniffled, like she was about to cry.

Sarah and Marco shared a look. He lifted and lowered a shoulder and snuggled down in his bedding. Yvonna knelt beside Cash. "It's been a really long day and I think the kids have been scared enough. They don't need to hear more strange things right before bed."

"But you believe me, right?" asked Cash. Her gaze darted to Sarah and then John. "I'm telling the truth. He kept me prisoner."

"Who?" asked Sarah. "Did you see him?"

"Not exactly." Cash swallowed. "But he spoke to me. And his voice was . . . weird. I couldn't exactly tell if it was male or female, but it seemed more male."

Marco sat back up. "What did he say?"

Cash frowned. "He said, 'I am a . . . collector. I am the curator of this place, you might say.' "

Goose bumps rose on Sarah's arms. What *exactly* did the Curator collect? Even if Cash was making it all up, it was downright spooky.

Cash continued, "I began to wonder what that place was. And if I was there to be part of his collection." Her voice lowered to a whisper. "Or if I already was."

John dropped a water bottle and Sarah shrieked. He rolled his eyes. "Okay, this is enough. Everyone is going to sleep, now!"

Yvonna said, "John, they'll never sleep. We'd better let Cash finish."

"Thank you." Cash smiled at Yvonna. "I told myself I wouldn't eat anything else. Maybe not eating would force him to let me go. But I got hungry. And the next time I ate, I felt all woozy. And I passed out."

"They drugged you?" asked Nacho.

Marco let out a huge sigh. "Like we didn't see that coming."

Nacho kicked at him. "Stop it. I believe her." He nodded at Cash. "Go on."

Cash hesitated, then went on. "When I woke up, I couldn't think straight. My head hurt. I reached up, but my hands were tied."

Cash reached down to rub one of her wrists. The light was too dim for Sarah to see if there were actually any marks. Her gaze flicked up to Cash's face. Maybe she was making it up. Maybe she was a great actress. But the look on her face was definitely one of fear.

Cash said, "The ceiling above me was made of rock. Like I was in a cave. I tried to kick, but my legs were tied too. I lifted my head enough to see someone in a blue jumpsuit dragging me by my feet."

"Dragging you where?" asked Nacho.

Cash shook her head. "I don't know. But I managed to get my hands loosened. And when he stopped to rest, he let go of my feet. I untied them and began to run. But then . . . " She stopped talking.

Sarah had begun to half believe Cash. She knew it

was farfetched and weird, but she'd seen things too, things nobody would believe. Softly, Sarah asked, "What happened?"

Cash met her gaze. "There was this huge *boom*. Rocks started falling down. So I just started running. The rough ground hurt my bare feet, but I just wanted to get out of there. So I saw a light and ran toward it."

"What was the light?" asked Sarah. "Where did you end up?"

Cash smiled. "The beach. I was so thankful to have soft sand under my feet." The smile left her face as quickly as it came. "But then I looked farther down the shoreline and there was this—" She made a circle with her hands. "I know you won't believe me, but there was this thing. This big round red ball in the sky, like a meteor or something. It came right for me, so I ran into the trees."

No one said anything.

Cash stared down at her hands. "I know y'all don't believe me."

Sarah reached out a hand and rested it on Cash's knee. "We saw it too. It's why we came to this cave."

Cash's shoulders relaxed. "You saw it?"

Marco and Nacho both nodded. Yvonna moved closer to John and he put his arm around her.

Cash shrugged. "That's about it. I ran to the beach

here and I saw your camp. I started to write a warning in the sand, and I guess that's when I collapsed." Her voice sounded hoarse again.

No one said a word. Sarah's dad and Yvonna exchanged a worried glance.

Sarah stared at her hand, frozen mid-stroke on Ahab's head. The red-orb-in-the-sky part was true, she'd seen it with her own eyes. Did that mean the rest was also the truth? Had Cash been a prisoner?

Sarah asked, "So the message in the sand. Beware the—"

Cash's eyes rose to meet hers. "I was trying to warn you. About the Curator."

A chill ran down Sarah's spine. Ahab nudged her hand with his nose. Sarah began petting him again, but noticed her hand was trembling.

"Well," said John. "I think we should all get ready for bed."

Everyone went outside for a bathroom break, and to brush their teeth with small cups of water. Then they settled down, no one saying a word. Sarah snuggled in, Ahab between her and Cash. Except for the blue glow from her dad's watch, the cave was black. Soon, she heard a few snores, and then, more deep, even breathing.

Still, Sarah couldn't sleep.

On the other side of Ahab, Cash let out a deep, ragged sigh.

Sarah reached out, making sure that Ahab was still there. Her hand landed in his soft, plush fur. She whispered to Cash, "You were lucky to escape."

"Was I?" Cash was quiet for a moment. "I mean, technically I didn't. I'm still stuck on this island." And in a whisper, she added, "And so are y'all."

Sarah's heart pounded a little faster. She scrunched her eyes shut and thought about California. She thought about her home and her room and her friends. She wondered whether she'd ever make it back, and found herself wishing she was already there.

4

Marco switched on his flashlight. The cave was so dark that anything not in the direct beam remained only a dim, colorless shape. He pointed the light at Nacho. His eyes were shut, his short hair stood straight up. Marco waggled the flashlight, but his brother didn't move.

Then he moved the beam to Sarah. Half her long hair had come loose from her ponytail and was puffed out around her face. She sat up and squinted in the light, then yawned and stretched out her arms, nearly colliding with Cash, who was also awake and stretching.

Cash didn't look as haggard as she had the day before, and she held a hand in front of her face to thwart the light. Then Marco swept the beam and caught the empty bedding where his mom and John had slept. Marco grabbed Nacho's shoulder and shook it gently. "Hey, let's go."

They gathered up all the bedding so they could carry it, then Nacho, Marco, and Sarah grabbed their backpacks. The four of them trooped outside, where the sun was still fairly low, a glowing peach in the pinkish eastern sky.

Cash yawned.

"Did you sleep okay?" Marco asked.

Cash nodded. "Better than I've slept since I got here." Her voice sounded much less hoarse.

Sarah asked, "Where's my dad?" She glanced around and called out, "Ahab?"

Marco shrugged. "Mom's not here either."

"Maybe they went to get the fire going," said Nacho. He dropped his load of bedding, then lifted his arms over his head and stretched, a huge yawn distorting his face.

"Probably." But Marco found it strange that their parents would leave them. "Let's head to the beach."

"What's that way?" Cash pointed to the left, toward the small house that Marco and John had found.

Marco's shoulders tensed and he quickly shook his head. "Nothing." He tried to keep a neutral expression on his face.

But Sarah stared at him. She asked, "That's where the house is, isn't it?"

"There's a house?" asked Cash.

"Yeah! Let's go to the house," said Nacho. "Maybe that's where Mom went."

Marco scowled. "I doubt it." He pointed the other way. "I really think we need to go to the beach."

Before Marco could stop him, Nacho jogged off in the direction of the cabin, his backpack bouncing up and down on his back. Cash shot a look at Marco and Sarah. She raised her eyebrows, then piled the pillows she carried on top of Nacho's bedding and followed him.

"Wait!" called Marco.

Sarah set a hand on his arm. "They just want to see it." She lifted and lowered a shoulder. "*I* want to see it." She dropped her hand. "It'll just be a quick look, okay?"

Marco nodded.

"You can stay here, if you want," she added.

"We should stay together." They both set their loads down and started walking. Marco heard a yelp up ahead and couldn't tell whether it was good or bad. He broke into a run. He heard Sarah behind him, and they emerged in the clearing a few moments later, breathing hard.

Cash was nowhere in sight, but Nacho stood on the front porch, his arms out to the sides, jumping up and down. He stopped when he saw them and blurted, "This is awesome! We should stay here from now on."

Marco asked him, "Where's Cash?"

Nacho gestured at the open door and headed through it, vanishing right as Marco yelled, "No! Don't go in there." He huffed in frustration and stomped over to the steps. "Nacho! Get out here."

Nacho reappeared, pouting. "Why? I just want to see inside."

"Me too," said Sarah, who had climbed up the steps. "Only for a couple minutes, then we can head to the beach."

Marco realized he couldn't keep them out, so he said, "At least let me go first." He stepped inside, Nacho at his back.

"Cobwebs," said Nacho. He made a face.

Sarah sneezed. "And dust."

Cash was stooped over the bed, running her hand over the embroidered scalloped edges of the linens. She turned her head toward them, an odd expression on her face.

"Something wrong?" asked Marco.

Cash straightened up. "Those are the same."

"Same as what?" asked Sarah.

Cash's gaze slipped to the bed once more. "As when the Curator held me prisoner." She sighed and crossed her arms. "It's the same material."

Goose bumps rose on Marco's arms. He wasn't sold on the Curator story, but her own conviction spooked him. "So what are you saying?"

"Nothing." Cash shook her head. "I'm not saying anything, other than"—she pointed at the bed—"those are the same sheets."

Sarah said, "Do you think the Curator stayed here?"

Marco said, "I think we should go now."

No one argued. Nacho was the first to zip out the door, followed closely by everyone else. Nacho stopped, opened his backpack, and removed a bottle of hand sanitizer. "Anyone?"

Three hands shot out.

Nacho held the bottle over Sarah's hand first and squeezed. The entire top blew off, and sanitizer quickly oozed out.

"Oh!" Nacho put his hand under it to try and catch some, but most of it was already on the ground. He held the bottle up. "It's almost gone." His forehead wrinkled.

Marco set a hand on his shoulder. "You have more."

"No I don't!" Nacho shook his head. "You made me leave my big bottles at home!" Tears welled up. "You said we would be able to buy more when I ran out!"

Marco held up his hands. "How was I supposed to know we'd get marooned?"

Cash stepped forward and put a hand on Nacho's shoulder. "Sarge says that stuff is bad for you anyway. Your body gets so used to not having any germs that when you do finally get some, it doesn't remember how to fight them off."

"Well, I guess we'll find out, *won't we*?" Nacho glared at Marco, then sniffled as he shoved the nearly empty bottle in his backpack.

Marco ignored him and led the way through the woods, Cash on his heels, Nacho and Sarah right behind. They stopped by the cave to retrieve the bedding, then set out for the beach. Marco heard Sarah ask Cash, "So, you're twelve?"

"Yeah," said Cash.

Sarah said, "Me too. So is Marco. His brother is only ten."

"I'm an only child," said Cash.

"Me too," said Sarah.

Marco frowned. Even though he didn't really think of her as his sister, that kind of felt like an insult.

Nacho quietly said, "Not anymore. Now you have us."

Sarah added, "Well, I meant that I used to be, I guess. They only got married like a month ago, so this is a new thing."

Again, Marco didn't appreciate the way Sarah sounded so flip, like she was dismissing him and Nacho as a temporary novelty. He wasn't that thrilled with her either, but she was, at least on paper, his stepsister.

As they emerged from the trees onto the beach, they

saw the fire blazing. Then, over by the monkey pod trees, Marco saw his mom and John with a stack of long bamboo stalks. Marco dropped the bedding and his backpack on the ground by the fire and jogged over. "What's going on?"

John looked up, a smile on his face. "I found a stand of bamboo." He rapped on one of the thick green poles with the knuckles of one hand. "Way better building material than trying to use the wood from the boat." He wrapped a braided rope of vines around a pole and attached it to a large square of bamboo that looked almost the size of a raft.

He pointed at a small machete. "This was in the dinghy. Luckily, it wasn't wet long enough to rust. I'm going to go cut some more in a bit."

Marco asked, "You want me to come with you?"

His mom said, "No. You are not touching that machete."

Marco stepped closer.

She was braiding several vines into a thick rope.

John said, "As soon as I get these secured together, we can lift them into the tree. We can make a fairly sturdy platform up there for the bedding. Then we'll have a safe place at night by the beach."

Marco smiled. He was stoked they wouldn't have to stay in the creepy house *or* the dank cave.

John asked, "How's the girl doing?"

"Fine, I think," said Marco.

"She has quite an imagination," John said.

Marco asked, "What do you mean?"

Yvonna said, "Her stories from last night. I think I believe how she came to be here, at least part of it, but that second part . . ." She shook her head.

"But we saw the red orb in the sky too," he said.

"Yes, but the rest . . . A curator, keeping her prisoner?" She shook her head. "I think she likes to tell stories and we were certainly a captive audience."

Marco's stomach lurched. He knew he had to tell them the truth, about everything he'd seen so far. "Mom, I have to tell you something."

John crossed his arms and leaned against the trunk of the nearest tree.

Marco looked at him. "You remember in the house? When I saw that bird?"

John nodded.

"It wasn't a normal bird. It had four wings and a mouth, with teeth."

John smiled. "Oh, come on. You trying to outdo the stories we heard last night?"

"And I found this." He reached into his pocket and pulled out the small bottle. He handed it to his mom.

Her eyes narrowed. "What's this?"

He said, "Just open it."

She twisted the pyramid-shaped stopper and sniffed. She began to smile at the smell, then her eyes widened. Slowly, she passed the bottle to John. He held it to his nose, then jerked it away. "What is this?"

Marco shrugged. "I don't know." He took the bottle back, put the top on, and shoved it deep into his pocket. "Sarah saw something weird too. A kangaroo."

"A what?" John looked at Yvonna. "That's not possible."

"Mom, something strange is going on here," said Marco. "That weird wail, and that red thing in the sky. Something is wrong with this place. Did you notice there aren't any birds?"

Yvonna and John looked up at the sky. She nodded. "I had noticed that."

Marco said, "I believe Cash. And I think you both should too."

John picked up the machete. "I think the only thing we should do right now is concentrate on getting this tree house built."

Marco realized he wasn't going to convince them all at once. And making a safe place for them to sleep at night was a good idea, he wouldn't argue that. He asked, "What can I do?"

His mom said, "Get everyone some breakfast first.

Then you can all help." She nodded at a mesh bag. "Take that over there. There's food in it."

"Okay." Marco carried the bag over to the others and set it by Nacho.

Cash sat cross-legged, staring into the flames. Nacho began to rustle through the bag of food. He seemed to have moved past his hand-sanitizer crisis of moments before. "Who's hungry?"

Marco asked, "What are the choices?"

Nacho stuck out his tongue. "I wasn't talking to you."

Marco rolled his eyes. Obviously, Nacho was not *quite* over his hand-sanitizer crisis after all.

Sarah said, "I kind of am." She looked at Cash, who nodded and said, "Yeah, me too."

Nacho pulled out a bunch of tiny yellow bananas. "We have these. And . . . ta-da!" He held up a box of Pop-Tarts.

Sarah's face lit up. "What kind?"

Nacho squinted at the box. "Raspberry."

"Nice," said Cash. "I'll take one please."

Nacho opened the box and handed her a silver packet. "Sarah?"

"I like the brown sugar ones better, but yeah. Hit me." She held out her hands and Nacho tossed a packet at her.

Marco sat down with the others.

Nacho began, "We should wash—" He stopped as

they all looked at him. "Force of habit, I guess." He shrugged.

Sarah said, "I'll walk with you to the water if you want to rinse your hands off."

Marco thought that was very nice of her, and decided to let his feelings over her "only child" comment from earlier go.

Nacho shook his head. "I'd better get used to it." He took a bite of his toaster pastry.

Marco pulled off a couple of bananas and peeled one.

Cash glanced around. "Y'all believe me, right? About everything?"

Marco met Sarah's gaze and whispered to her, "I told my mom and your dad everything."

Her eyes widened. "Did they believe you?"

He shrugged, then looked back at Cash. "Yeah. It all sounds really weird, but I think I do believe you. We've seen some weird stuff here." He told them about the red bird, then Sarah added in her kangaroo. Marco pulled the bottle out of his pocket. "And I found this in that house."

Nacho asked, "Today?" Apparently, he was talking to Marco again.

Marco shook his head. "When I was there the first time." He handed it to Nacho and then took a large bite of the banana.

Nacho pulled out the stopper and sniffed. "Wow, that smells—" His eyebrows knit together. "Who is that?"

Cash asked, "What?"

Nacho handed her the bottle, which she sniffed. Her eyes widened. "Bizarre." She quickly handed the bottle back to Nacho, who replaced the stopper and returned it to Marco.

Nacho asked, "Who do you think lived in that house?"

Marco shrugged. He finished the banana and peeled the other one.

"Do you think they're still here?" asked Nacho.

Marco took a bite and shook his head.

"Do you think they're coming back?" asked Nacho.

Marco and Sarah looked at each other. Sarah said, "Hopefully we'll get out of here before we even have to worry about that."

Marco finished chewing and swallowed. Half of the banana remained, but he tossed it into the fire. All of a sudden, he wasn't hungry anymore.

5

Sarah finished eating and stood up. "Anyone seen Ahab?" She stuck her fingers in her mouth and blew an ear-shattering whistle.

Nacho asked, "How'd you do that?"

Sarah shrugged. "I just taught myself." When Ahab didn't show, she put her hands on her hips. "Where is he?" She whistled again and Ahab pranced up from the direction of the beach, his fur wet. "Hey, boy!"

He shook himself before he reached them, and Sarah reached out to pet him. "Where were you?"

Marco stood up. "I'm gonna go help my mom with the tree house."

Since Sarah had finally seen the little house, and because it creeped her out, she decided that staying in it wasn't at the top of her list after all. And the cave had been so dark and damp. A tree house actually sounded appealing. “I’ll help too,” she said.

Nacho and Cash seemed content where they were.

Marco headed toward the monkey pod trees and Sarah followed, Ahab at her side. Her dad gave her a quick hug. “You two want to help me get the platform into the tree?”

They both nodded.

The three of them carried the bamboo square over to the tree and leaned it there. John said, “I’ll climb up there, then if you can lift it up to me, I can pull it the rest of the way.” He quickly climbed the biggest monkey pod tree, so that he was about ten feet off the ground. “Okay, just lift from the bottom. Go straight up to me.”

Sarah squatted next to Marco as they both got a grip on the edge of the bamboo square. She straightened her legs and the square lifted up, so that the top edge reached her dad’s feet. He grabbed it and pulled. “Now push!”

Marco and Sarah shoved, and the bamboo square inched upward until it leveled and then was above their heads. Sarah watched as her dad maneuvered it into place, edges resting on both of the trees. He pounded on it with his hand. “Seems solid. But here’s the real test.”

He put a foot on it and pushed a little.

Yvonna came and stood next to Sarah. She called up, “Be careful!”

John smiled down at them. "Don't you trust my engineering skills?"

Sarah held her breath as her dad stepped onto the platform. It didn't budge. She clapped. "You did it!"

Her dad moved back over to the tree. "This is enough room for the three girls to sleep. Now we can start working on the boys' side."

Marco asked, "What if someone rolls off?"

John shook his head. "I'll rig up some railings. Nobody will fall off." He climbed back down and picked up the machete. "I'm going to cut more bamboo. You two help Yvonna with the vines."

Sarah didn't like the idea of her dad going off alone. She asked, "You want to take Ahab?"

"Sure." He pointed down the beach. "If anyone needs me, the bamboo stand is down the beach a ways, then I cut into the trees." He and Ahab headed down toward the water, and soon disappeared around the corner.

Sarah and Marco sat on either side of Yvonna. She handed them each a handful of long vines. "Take several and separate them into three groups, then braid."

Sarah started in on the task, but Yvonna suddenly put a hand to her mouth.

"Mom?" asked Marco. "Are you—"

Yvonna got to her feet and lurched into the trees.

Sarah heard her throwing up. She frowned and asked Marco, "Is she sick?"

He shrugged. "She's been sick for a couple days now."

"When? She seemed fine to me," said Sarah.

"It's not all the time," Marco said. "She'll be okay."

They kept working on their ropes, and a few minutes later, Yvonna came out of the trees, staggering a bit.

Marco jumped up. "Mom!" He ran to her just as she began to fall. He held her up, and Sarah quickly went to help.

Yvonna said, "I'm feeling a little woozy. Maybe I should sit for a few minutes."

They helped her over to one of the tree trunks, and she sat down, leaning back against it. Her face was sweaty.

Sarah got a bottle of water and brought it to her. "Here."

"Thank you," said Yvonna. She took a sip, and then breathed out. "Probably the heat getting to me." She shut her eyes.

"Do you want me to go get my dad?" asked Sarah.

Yvonna shook her head. "No, I'll be fine."

Sarah went over to the fire. Nacho and Cash were poking sticks in the flames. Nacho asked, "What are you guys doing?"

"Making ropes out of vines," she said. Sarah picked up a blanket and a couple of pillows.

"What are those for?" asked Nacho.

Sarah sighed, wondering if she should say anything. "To lean against the tree while we work."

Neither Cash nor Nacho said anything else, so Sarah headed back. She told Yvonna, "Here, lean forward." She stuck the pillows between Yvonna and the tree. Then she folded up the blanket and stuck it under Yvonna's feet.

"Thank you, sweetie," mumbled Yvonna. Her eyes were closed.

Marco looked worried, and Sarah whispered, "Should we get my dad?"

"I don't know," he said. "Maybe she'll be fine once she gets some rest."

Sarah nodded and sat back down. "Do you think everyone believed what you told them?"

Marco shrugged. "I didn't hold back anything, that's for sure. The bird, the bottle. Your kangaroo. I don't know if they believed me. I mean, they were a little freaked by the bottle, but I don't know if it was enough to convince them that Cash's story was true."

Sarah asked, "Do you think it is?"

"After everything?" Marco frowned. "Mostly I guess. I mean we've seen some weird stuff here. The whole thing about the Curator though? That seemed a little . . . strange."

"Even though the sheets at the house were the same as where she was imprisoned?" asked Sarah.

"We don't know if that's true or if she made it up," said Marco.

Suddenly, Yvonna got on her knees and crawled a few yards away. Sarah heard her throw up again.

"What's wrong with Mom?" Nacho was there, right behind them.

Marco stood up. "Duh, she's sick."

"Why didn't you tell me?" Nacho smacked Marco's arm. "I'm her kid too."

Marco said, "Because there's nothing you can do about it."

Yvonna stood and walked back over to them. "Sorry, guys. I can't seem to stop throwing up." She sighed and pressed a hand to her forehead. "My head feels a little better though." She leaned down and picked up the pillows and blanket. "I'm going to lie down over there." She pointed about twenty yards away, where another monkey pod tree had a big pool of shade under it. "Just to get a little quiet. Keep working on the ropes; John will want them when he comes back with the bamboo."

"Are you okay?" asked Nacho.

She nodded and set a hand on his head, then slowly walked off.

Sarah picked up the bottle of water. "She needs to stay hydrated." She ran after Yvonna and handed her the bottle of water.

"Here. You need to drink."

Yvonna took it. "Thanks. I know, I'm trying to keep some down." She sighed. "You'd think I'd be used to this."

Sarah walked beside her. "Used to what?"

Yvonna shook her head. "Nothing." She reached the tree and started to spread the blanket out, but Sarah took care of it, and set the pillows down. Yvonna slowly dropped to her knees and then laid her head down on the pillows. She closed her eyes. "I'll be over in a bit," she said. "I just need a little nap, I think."

"Take your time," said Sarah. She walked back to the boys under the monkey pod trees. Cash joined them. Sarah sat down and picked up her vine, thinking as she braided. She did hope Yvonna was okay. And she hoped her dad got back very soon.

6

Marco couldn't help glancing over at his mom under the tree, hoping she would be fine. And he appreciated Sarah being nice to her. He whispered, "Thanks for that."

Sarah nodded. "Of course. I hope she feels better."

The four of them worked hard at their task without speaking for a few moments. Then Nacho asked Cash, "So when do you think Sarge will come back?"

"I don't know." Cash held her vines still in her lap for a moment. "Fox has to find his treasure first."

Sarah looked up. "Treasure? I thought it was cargo?"

Cash froze. "Well, yeah. It is cargo. I mean, I guess I just accidentally called it that."

Again, Marco wondered whether she was keeping something from them. Did she know what Fox was looking for? Other than the landmark—the face rock—did she know something else? What the cargo—or treasure—was? And if she did, why had she kept that from them?

Or maybe her entire story was fake and she would keep making mistakes as she forgot what versions she told.

Cash shrugged. "It doesn't really matter, right? I mean, this island isn't the one he was looking for. He said that himself. Once they do find it, Sarge will come back to get me and that'll be that. We can all get off the island then." She stuck a Pop-Tart in her mouth and took a big bite.

Nacho said, "It could be gold coins or something! That would be cool."

The talk of treasure made Marco remember the trunk from the sailboat. He glanced over at the pile of things from the boat. He needed something to distract the others, and he knew just the thing. "You guys want to see something cool?"

Sarah said, "Only if it isn't alive."

Marco smiled. "Nope. I promise."

He stood up. At first, he didn't see what he was looking for. Then he remembered that he'd draped a burlap sack over it when they first arrived. He swept aside the burlap, revealing the trunk.

"Oh, I saw that on the beach before," said Sarah.

"Where did it come from?" She and the others set their vines aside and joined Marco.

"It was on *Moonflight,*" said Marco. "Belonged to Captain Norm, I guess. We rescued it from the boat, thinking maybe we could get it back to his family or something." He didn't add that he hoped he would be able to keep it when this adventure was all over.

"Where do you think he got it?" asked Nacho. "It is so awesome."

In the sun, the dark wood looked lighter and shinier, showing more details of the intricately carved scenes. The colorful abalone inlays sparkled as Sarah and Nacho ran their hands over them.

"They're so smooth," said Sarah. "This mermaid's eyes look like rubies."

Marco stepped closer. Writing ran around the lid of the trunk, but not in any letters he recognized. He wondered what language it was, and why he hadn't noticed it before, but the light in the cabin of the boat had been dim.

Sarah asked, "Is that Latin or something?"

Marco shrugged.

"Check out the sea serpent!" said Nacho. He peered more closely, his nose nearly touching the front of the trunk. "His teeth look sharp." He ran his fingers over the sea serpent's mouth. "Ow!" He jerked his hand back. "They are sharp."

Marco laughed. "What do you think?" he asked Cash.

But she just stood there in a daze, staring at the trunk with her mouth half open.

Marco said, "Cash?"

"Huh?" Her eyes snapped back into focus and she smiled quickly. "It's cool." She stepped forward and ran her hand over the inlay of a ship. "Really cool."

Marco frowned as he watched the three inspect the outside of the trunk. Cash was acting weird. Like she recognized the trunk. Had she seen it before? Or maybe . . . had someone told her about it?

She turned to him and asked, "Can we open it?"

"Yeah!" said Nacho. "Let's open it!"

"No!" snapped Marco, before he could stop himself. For a moment, he wished he had kept the trunk to himself and not shown them. They all acted as if it was community property and belonged to them as well. He didn't like it. "I mean, no. I tried before. It won't open."

Nacho knelt in front of the trunk and inspected the latch. He pushed it and rapped his knuckles on it. He shook his head. "I think we need a key or something."

Cash asked, "What about a knife? Do y'all have one of those around here?"

Sarah started to say, "Yeah, over—"

"Just stop." Marco interrupted her. "All of you. We're not going to wreck it just to see what's inside."

Nacho wrinkled his nose at Marco. "Who put you in charge?"

Marco jabbed a thumb at his own chest. "I found it. I dragged it off the boat."

"My dad helped, probably," said Sarah. Then she shrugged. "But you're right." She ran a hand over the top of the trunk. "It's too pretty to mess with. Maybe there isn't even anything in there."

Nacho looked disappointed. "Whatever." He sat back down and picked up his vines.

Sarah sat down too.

Cash's gaze lingered on the trunk for a beat too long before she turned and joined them.

Marco watched her for a moment. Then he retrieved the burlap bag and carefully covered up the trunk before joining the others. He finished his vine and began another.

Sarah said, "Captain Norm believed in mermaids."

"Huh?" asked Marco.

Sarah nodded. "He told me about it. When he was young he sailed in the Caribbean and he met sailors who believed they saw mermaids."

Marco made a face. "You're kidding."

Sarah shook her head, "No, I'm serious! So maybe he thought the trunk was some kind of mermaid thing. With some kind of mermaid magic."

Nacho said, "Mermaids aren't magic."

Cash asked, "How do you know?"

Nacho said, "The aquatic ape theory."

Marco laughed. "What are you talking about?"

"Seriously," said Nacho. "I saw it on Animal Planet."

Cash rolled her eyes at Sarah, who asked, "What did it say?"

"Well, the theory is kinda cool." Nacho got a serious look on his face. "So like millions of years ago, there was a lot of flooding along the coasts of all the land on Earth. Half our ancestors went inland, but half went into the water."

"Ancestors?" Marco raised his eyebrows. "Like cavemen?"

Nacho shook his head. "Probably older than that. More like ape ancestors."

Sarah shook her head and concentrated on her rope. "I don't believe it."

"You don't have to." Nacho smiled at her. "It's just a theory. Anyway, the ones that went in the water adapted. And the theory is that's where the mermaids came from: a branch of evolution that went into the water."

Sarah said, "You know how ridiculous that sounds, right? Apes in the water?"

"Maybe." Nacho shrugged. "But here's the really cool part. There are lots of things about us modern people, which back up the theory that we once lived in the ocean. One." He held up a finger. "Humans are the only primates with webbing between the fingers."

Marco glanced down at his hands and spread them out. He was pretty sure that the slight webbing could be explained in any number of ways *other* than that the human race used to live in the ocean.

Nacho held up another finger. "Two. Humans have way less body hair than other primates. It would have created drag in the water."

"Olympic swimmers do shave their whole bodies," said Cash.

Nacho held up another finger. "Three. Humans are the only land animals with a layer of the same fat that helps insulate dolphins and whales." Another finger. "Four. Humans can hold their breath longer than any other land animal. Oh! And five." He snapped up his thumb. "We're the only land animal with an instinctive ability to swim."

"Other land animals can swim," said Marco.

"Yeah," said Nacho. "But it's not as natural as it is with humans."

Sarah and Cash exchanged a glance. Marco didn't

want them to make fun of Nacho, so he said, "Well, it's just a theory. Interesting anyway." He wanted to get off the subject, so he asked, "Anybody want to help me start tying the bamboo together? Maybe there's enough to make another platform."

7

About an hour later, they had several ropes made and another group of bamboo poles tied together. The rectangle was big enough to fit across the remaining space between the trees. Sarah said, "Let's get it up there before my dad gets back. We'll surprise him."

"I think we should wait," said Nacho. "That's pretty high up."

Marco shook his head. "No it's not. We'll just connect vines to it, like a pulley, and I'll go up there and reel it in." He climbed up to the platform already there and sat on it. His feet dangled over the edge. "Okay, hook the vine in between two poles and secure it."

Cash and Sarah did as he asked, then Nacho helped them lift it up as Marco strained to pull it. "You guys gotta hold it higher!"

Sarah grunted as she shoved the platform higher. What did he expect from them? She yelled, "We're trying!"

"You're the one that wanted to do this before your dad got back!" snapped Marco.

Sarah made a face at him. But he was right. "Fine," she said. "Let's do it."

Marco leaned back for more leverage and managed to get the edge of the bamboo over the platform already in place. He grabbed hold of the edge and said, "Okay, now just push it a little more."

"We are!" said Nacho.

"On three," said Cash. "One big push."

Sarah adjusted her hands that were hurting from holding on to the bamboo for so long. "Okay. Ready."

Cash said, "One. Two. Three!"

Groaning, the three of them shoved the platform as Marco pulled, and enough of it got over the edge that it tipped up and out of their grip.

"You got it?" called Sarah, crossing her fingers. Marco was hidden by the bamboo.

"Yeah!" called Marco. The bamboo went flat and he was visible again, kneeling on the platform.

Sarah stepped back so she could see what he was doing. He set the new section of platform in place next to the other, then leaned over the side with a wide grin. "It's perfect. Just hand me some vines so I can tie it into place."

Cash already had a handful of rope, and tossed it up.

Nacho said, "Here. I made something." His arms were full of vines. But with a flourish, he flung them out, hanging on to the very end.

"A ladder?" asked Sarah.

"That's so cool," said Cash.

"Will it work?" Marco was gazing at them, his face shiny with sweat from the exertion.

Nacho nodded. "Let's try it."

Marco reached down as Nacho tossed up the end of it. Marco secured the top of the ladder with more braided vines, then unrolled the rest of it, so it wavered in the air. "Who wants to be first?"

Nacho looked skeptical.

Sarah didn't want him to feel bad if the ladder didn't work. Maybe it would work for her, since she was so light. She raised her hand. "I'll do it." She kicked off her flip-flops and grabbed ahold of the nearest vine rung, which was about at chest level. "I might need a boost."

Cash came up behind her and said, "Here, let me give you a piggyback."

Sarah climbed up on Cash's back, grabbed a higher rung, and managed to get one of her bare feet onto the lowest rung. Then she slowly began to climb.

The vines cut into her hands and feet, but not too badly. She quickly reached the top where Marco took her arm and pulled her up onto the platform. She sat there and caught her breath as she looked around. To be up that high in the tree on such a wide, sturdy platform made her feel safe. She smiled.

Marco grinned. "It's cool, huh?"

She nodded at him. "Let's get the mattresses up here."

The mattresses were smaller, and not quite as unwieldy as the bamboo had been. The four of them managed to pad the platform within half an hour. Cash and Nacho tossed up pillows and blankets, and Sarah quickly made a cozy nest of the space. She plumped up one last pillow and arranged it with the others. "There."

"It looks great," said Marco. "Way better than the cave."

Sarah pointed at the branch where she spent the night the crabs invaded. "Or my perch." Sweat dripped down her face and she wiped it off. "I'm thirsty."

"Me too," said Marco. He went down the ladder, then Sarah followed. She jumped the final three feet or so, landing in the sand. She brushed herself off and accepted the bottle of water Nacho handed her. "Thanks."

Cash was wiping sweat off her face. "I'm so hot." She gazed down at the beach. "I want to swim, but the salt water makes my hair all stiff and salty."

"Mine too," said Sarah.

Marco said, "I know where we can swim. And it's fresh water." He reached into a canvas bag and pulled out a bottle of shampoo. "And you can even wash your hair."

Sarah didn't want to leave the safety of their camp. She wanted to wait for her dad. But swimming, getting clean, and being refreshed? That sounded way too good to pass up. She took the bottle from Marco, picked up a towel off the pile from the boat and said, "Show us where to go."

8

Marco went to check on his mom. She was asleep and he wondered whether leaving her was a good idea. But he was so sweaty and hot. Cooling off in fresh water was too tempting. She would be fine if they weren't gone too long.

He grabbed a towel off the pile. "Okay, anybody got a watch?"

Nacho raised his wrist.

"What time is it?" Marco asked.

"Ten," said Nacho.

"We have to be back by eleven, okay?" Marco glanced back at his mom once more. "I don't want to leave her more than an hour."

"My dad might be back before then. Should we leave a note?" asked Sarah.

Marco shook his head. "He'll figure we're just looking for food or something. Besides, we'll be back soon." He started off toward the trees, everyone falling in behind him. He set a fast pace, not wanting to waste all their time walking, in order to leave plenty of time for swimming. He was tired, and didn't feel like talking. Apparently no one else did either. Their footsteps, and the occasional swish of foliage as they brushed past, were the only sounds he heard.

They reached the clearing with the house, but Marco walked right past without giving it a glance. Now that they had the platform in the trees, they had no use for the building. He turned the corner at the side of the house and stopped at the curtain of vines.

"I hear water," said Nacho.

Sarah nodded.

Cash said, "Me too."

Marco swept aside the vines and stepped through, holding them up for the others. Sarah gasped as she walked past Marco, stopping at the edge of the crystal-clear stream. "It's beautiful," she said.

Cash squealed. "Look at the fruit trees!" She stood under a mango tree, gazing up.

Marco stopped beside her and reached down on the ground for one that looked perfectly ripe and not too bruised from the fall. He set down his towel and took his knife out of his pocket. "This will be a little messy, but . . ." He cut off the peel and handed the skinned slippery orange fruit to Cash.

She held it to her mouth and bit into it. The juice dripped down her face as she grinned. "Delicious."

Marco grabbed a few more and put them in his towel. "Let's go."

"Wait." Nacho had his towel tucked under his arm, a fat, dark green avocado in each hand. He held one to Marco. "Can you cut it open for me?"

Marco sliced the avocado in two, popped out the pit, and handed one half back to Nacho.

"Hey," said Nacho.

"We can get more," said Marco. He put the other half in his mouth, scraping out the insides with his teeth. *Delicious.*

Sarah was kneeling by the stream, splashing water on her face. Marco said, "Come on, we're almost there." He led the way around the corner as the sound of rushing water got louder. He turned to see the reaction of the others as the waterfall came into view.

Cash's eyes widened as Sarah set a hand over her mouth. Nacho yelled, "Oh yeah!" He tossed his towel on the ground, followed by one avocado and what remained of the other. He tore off his T-shirt and jumped in the water. Out of sight for several seconds, his head popped back up, a wide grin on his face. "Awesome!"

Cash kicked off her flip-flops, pitched the rest of the mango into the bushes, and jumped into the pool fully clothed. She popped back up, sputtering.

"You okay?" yelled Marco.

She nodded, laughing. "Colder than I thought."

Sarah set her flip-flops next to her towel, then sat on the bank and let her feet sink into the water. "Nice."

Marco took off his shirt and dropped it on the ground with his towel. "You going in?" he asked.

"In a minute." She kicked her feet, splashing. "Just taking my time."

"We're on a schedule, you know." And before she could react, Marco put both his hands on her back and shoved her in the water. She bobbed back up, scowling. "I was going to go in on my own time, you know!"

Marco laughed and cannonballed next to her. He heard her screech even though he was still underwater. He surfaced, then took a face full of water as she splashed him. "Hey!" he called.

She laughed. "I owed you."

"Where's that shampoo?" called Cash.

Sarah grabbed it from the bank and pushed off from the bottom, bouncing her way over to Cash. The two squirted shampoo into their hands and quickly sudsed up their heads. Marco went over for some, and called out to Nacho, "Dude, you should wash your hair too. Don't know when we'll get a chance again."

Nacho splashed around a bit before he complied, but within ten minutes of getting in the water, all four had dripping, fresh-smelling hair. Marco threw the bottle of shampoo onto the bank.

"What was that?" asked Cash.

Marco froze. Nacho was still splashing, and Marco slashed a hand across his throat. Nacho stopped and stood still, water dripping down his face.

There was a crashing in the underbrush, loud enough to be heard over the waterfall. Marco said, "Let's get out."

Sarah and Cash quickly scrambled up the bank and grabbed their towels. Nacho was farther away. He began to swim toward Marco, when there was a flash of black fur in the woods. Marco reached out and grabbed his brother, then waved at the girls, motioning for them to hide.

They ducked behind a large rock. Marco put a finger to his lips and led Nacho to the side of the water. There, they ducked lower than the bank, hopefully out of sight of whatever was there.

The waterfall continued to rush. Right above them, Marco heard chuffing. The girls were still out of sight behind the rock. Finally, the sound went away. Marco waited another moment, just to be sure, then he stepped out from the bank a tad to look into the underbrush. Nothing. He let out the breath he didn't know he'd been holding. He took Nacho's arm and said, "Come on. We better get back."

They quickly dried off and headed back to the fruit trees, where they stopped to pick some more for the camp. Then, towels laden and heavy and damp, they headed back to the beach, Marco glancing back every now and then, wondering whether there had been something back there. And whether it had seen them.

9

They walked in silence. Sarah felt cooler and cleaner. She couldn't stop lifting and dropping strands of her hair in front of her face in order to smell the lovely scent of shampoo. She'd always taken being clean for granted and decided then and there to never do that again. Marco was up ahead, walking faster than she felt like. She hadn't seen anything at the pool when they hid; maybe there had been something, maybe there hadn't. She wished they could have stayed longer.

Marco asked Nacho, "What time is it?"

"Almost eleven," said Nacho.

"Do you think my dad is back yet?" asked Sarah.

"He should be," said Marco. "I mean, it's been a while and he was just going to get bamboo."

Sarah increased her pace. "He's probably there and wondering where we are."

"Will he get mad?" asked Cash.

Sarah shook her head. "Probably just worried enough to give me a lecture." Her stomach growled. "I'm ready for some lunch."

They emerged from the trees and headed over to their camp. Yvonna stood there, waving at them. But to Sarah, she looked no better than before.

Yvonna asked, "Where did you kids go?"

"Swimming!" called Nacho.

"Nice." But the corners of Yvonna's mouth barely curled. "Is John with you?"

Sarah shook her head. "I thought he'd be here by now." Why wasn't he back yet?

"Don't worry," said Marco. "He probably wanted to get as much cut as he could."

Yvonna put her face in her hands.

"Mom?" asked Nacho. "You okay?"

She took her hands away. "I just feel so weak." Then she quickly turned and stepped into the trees, sick once again.

Cash asked, "What's wrong with her?"

Sarah glanced at Marco, whose forehead was all wrinkled. She set a hand on his arm. "She'll be okay."

Marco asked, "How do you know?"

But Sarah didn't know. She didn't know anything. She was simply trying to be nice because it felt like the right thing to do.

Nacho pulled out his notebook. "What if she gets dehydrated?" He read a little bit, then lifted his head. In a tone drenched with authority, he barked, "We need coconuts."

Sarah pointed at the small pile of brown ones that remained. "There's some."

Nacho shook his head. "We need the raw ones, the drinking nuts. They're big and green. They have juice in them that will be really good for Mom." He replaced the notebook in his backpack.

Yvonna came out of the trees, her hair disheveled. Her steps were uneven, and Marco jumped up and ran over to her. "Mom?" He put his arm around her and she leaned on him.

He called out, "Somebody get the pillows and blanket."

"I will!" said Cash. She ran over to the tree where Yvonna had been resting.

Sarah went to help Marco with Yvonna. Together, they got her over to the camp and waited for Cash to spread the blanket before lowering Yvonna down.

She immediately fell back on the pillows, a hand over her eyes.

Sarah said, "You should drink some water."

Yvonna shook her head. "I can't. I will in a minute."

Sarah glanced at Marco. His mouth was a thin line, and his eyes were narrowed. She whispered, "She's got to drink something."

Marco said, "Maybe Nacho is right. We should find some of those drinking coconuts." He glanced around. "Where is he?"

Sarah turned. Nacho was nowhere. She asked Cash, "Where'd Nacho go?"

Cash shrugged. "I don't know. I was getting the pillows and stuff."

Marco put both hands on top of his head. "He probably went to find the coconuts himself." He sighed.

Sarah said, "I should go get my dad."

Marco nodded. "And I need to find Nacho." He looked at Sarah and pointed toward the beach. "We should go after them."

Cash's eyes widened and she shook her head so hard that her braids flew up. "No way. I'm not going that way."

Sarah said, "You can stay here."

"Yeah," said Marco. "Will you watch my mom?"

Cash nodded. "Of course." She glanced down at

Yvonna. "Although I don't know how much I can do for her."

Sarah said, "We shouldn't be gone long." She hoped, anyway. "But just in case, I'll get some supplies." She went over to the monkey pod trees and found a small blue canvas bag with a long white strap. She packed it with some fruit, a few bottles of water, and a flashlight. A paring knife fell off a pile of towels, and she tossed that in there too.

Marco came over and dug in his suitcase. He held up a pair of sneakers. "We'd better wear something other than flip-flops."

"Okay." Sarah's heart pounded at the idea of going off on their own, but she had to find her dad. Nothing would stop her from at least trying. She dug out her sneakers and put those on, then went back over to the group. She quickly put two braids in her hair. Then she stood up and asked Marco, "You ready?"

Marco nodded and sank to his knees beside his mom. "We'll be back as soon as we can. With John. And some coconut juice for you." He gave her a quick hug, then told Sarah, "Let's go."

10

As they walked along the beach, Marco hoped he wasn't making a mistake by leaving his mom alone. Technically, she wasn't alone—she had Cash—but Marco still worried about her.

Sarah said, "She'll be okay."

Marco glanced at her and nodded. "I know." He lifted and lowered his shoulder. "I still worry."

Sarah added, "And we'll find Nacho. He can't be far."

Marco smiled then. "He drives me crazy sometimes, but he's my little brother. I wouldn't ever want anything to happen to him."

"I get it," said Sarah. "Not that I know what it's like, but I like Nacho. He knows a lot. I mean that whole thing about the ape mermaids? Pretty crazy."

Marco said, "Yeah, he does know a lot."

Sarah smiled. "You sound surprised."

"Well, I—" He wasn't sure what was more unexpected: that she noticed his little brother was smart or that she admitted she liked him.

"What?" There was an edge to her voice.

"Nothing," said Marco, although he couldn't help but wonder how Sarah felt about him. He figured she still held a grudge because he hadn't told their parents about the red bird the first time she asked him to. "I'm glad you like him. I guess I didn't expect that. Some people might think he's a little obsessive. I mean, with the hand sanitizer and all."

Sarah raised her eyebrows. "I know a lot of people who use way more of that than he does. I use it all the time during flu season at school. And besides, what's not to like? He's pretty handy."

Marco smiled. "Yeah, I guess so."

Sarah said, "I think he likes Cash too. She's pretty nice."

"Yeah, I guess," said Marco.

Sarah looked at him. "What?"

He said, "I just thought it was weird when I showed the trunk to you guys. You and Nacho both had the same look on your faces, like you thought it was cool. But Cash . . ."

"I didn't notice," said Sarah. "What did she do?"

"I don't know," said Marco. "It was almost like she recognized it."

Sarah asked, "Do you think she's seen it before?"

"No. But I do think that she's heard about it before." Marco stopped and faced Sarah. "Remember how she told us about Fox's cargo? But then later, she slipped and called it treasure?"

Sarah nodded. "It could've been an honest mistake."

"Maybe," said Marco. "But I just got the feeling that maybe Fox spilled some details about his treasure, details which included that trunk."

Sarah frowned. "But, if that trunk is actually Fox's treasure, how did it end up on *Moonflight*?"

Marco shrugged and started walking again. "Captain Norm went all over these islands. There was like over a year after Fox got rescued before he went on the boat with Cash and Sarge."

"So you think Captain Norm found it on an island?" asked Sarah.

"Maybe," said Marco.

"But if he did," mused Sarah, "why didn't he open it?"

Marco shrugged. "Captain Norm seemed content with his life, don't you think? I mean, look at the condition of his boat. Maybe he appreciated the trunk for what it was on the outside."

Sarah frowned. "I don't think so. He was a businessman. I mean, he didn't even offer us a discount when we saw his boat wasn't anything like the one in the brochure." She shook her head. "He wouldn't have left the trunk alone because he was nice." She raised her eyebrows. "Maybe he thought it was cursed. If he believed in mermaids, he might have believed other things too."

"Why would he think that?" asked Marco.

"Maybe someone gave it to him, but with a warning." She shrugged. "He obviously didn't get into it. There had to be a reason."

Marco stopped walking. "Do you think we should go back? What if Cash tries to open it? I don't want her ruining it."

Sarah's eyes widened and she pointed ahead, to a trail that went into the dense trees. "Look."

Marco turned. "Maybe that's where your dad has been going."

Sarah breathed out. "Only one way to find out."

Marco led the way into the trees. The path was mostly dirt and not very wide, but seemed like it had been used a lot. Soon the trees thickened, shutting out some of the daylight, making it seem more like a rain forest with a cover above them.

"It's way cooler in here," commented Sarah.

"Yeah," said Marco. He wondered where the bamboo was.

Sarah said, "I could whistle for Ahab. I mean, if he's anywhere near us he'd hear and come running. Or at least bark."

Marco shook his head. "No. I don't think that's a good idea." He saw something shiny, half hidden in the dirt, and stooped to pick it up. A silver anchor, engraved with letters AHAB. He grinned and held it up. "Looks like we're on the right path." He handed it to Sarah.

Sarah squinted at the anchor. "Wait a second."

"It's Ahab's. I saw it on his collar." Marco didn't understand why she was acting so skeptical. "Your dad must have come this way with the dog."

Sarah shook her head. "The one Ahab has on is misspelled, with two *b*'s. Captain Norm told me Ahab had lost the one with the correct spelling"—she brandished the tag—"on an island." She looked around. "They were here before. On this island."

A soft chuffing made Marco freeze. "Did you hear that?

Sarah said, "Hear what?"

Marco lifted a finger to his lips, then jabbed it in the air to his left.

The chuffing grew louder.

Marco grabbed Sarah's arm and pulled her behind a tree with him. His heart pounded as they crouched there, listening as the chuffing turned into a loud crunching.

"Sounds like something is eating something," whispered Sarah.

The sound stopped. Marco put a finger to his lips. Sarah nodded.

Suddenly, there was a rush of leaves and a flash of gray. The ground shook so hard that they each grabbed a tree to keep their balance. A large something charged past them, gone before they could see what it was.

They brushed themselves off and then stepped out onto the path. "What was that?" Marco was panting, and his hands trembled.

Sarah's face was pale. "I don't know." She looked one way, then the other. "I don't even know which way it went."

Marco scratched his head. "Do we keep going?"

"Or should we go back?" asked Sarah.

Marco sighed. They had to find John and Nacho, but what were they getting themselves into? "I don't know."

Sarah still had the dog tag in her hand. She pinched it between two fingers and held it up. "Should we flip for it?"

Marco nodded. "Heads we go back and just wait for them to return. Tails we keep going."

Sarah tossed the tag and caught it, then flipped it

onto the back of her wrist. She slowly lifted her hand, revealing the blank side. She raised her eyebrows. "Looks like we keep going."

Marco swallowed, wondering what they were going to find as they headed farther into the trees.

11

Sarah followed Marco as he walked slowly along the path. She glanced furtively behind her every now and then, hoping nothing was going to creep up on them. She had no idea what had run by them, but that thing was big. Monstrous. She definitely didn't want to encounter it on this narrow path. "Do you think we're going the right way?"

Marco didn't turn around, but said, "I don't even know what the right way is."

Sarah said, "The right way is the way that will find my dad and Nacho and Ahab." Thinking of the dog made her wonder about Captain Norm. Obviously he had been to this island before. Was this the island he meant to take them to? "Do you think that . . ."

Marco called back over his shoulder, "What?"

"If this is the island Captain Norm meant to take us to, it would be on his float plan or whatever, right?" Sarah stumbled over a root and caught herself before she fell.

"Yeah, I guess," said Marco.

"So someone should be coming to rescue us, right?" She hoped Marco agreed, because it would make her feel better.

But his shoulders went up and down. "The whole thing seems sketchy to me. Like the regular rules of the world don't apply."

Sarah didn't say anything else as she kept on following him. She gazed around the area, checking for any signs that her dad might have come that way. Then Marco stopped and she ran right into him, hitting her mouth on his shoulder. "Ow." She put a hand up to her lip.

He set a hand on a tree to keep his balance and looked at her. "You okay?"

She moved her hand and pointed at her lip. "Am I bleeding?"

Marco squinted at where she pointed. "Don't think so. But check that out." He looked ahead of him.

The end of the path split into a V.

"Which way?" she asked.

Marco put his hands on his hips and shook his head. "I have no clue."

Sarah heard something. "Do you hear that?" The

sound she strained to hear grew louder and louder, until there was no doubt.

"Yeah, I hear it." Marco tilted his head to the side a bit and scrunched up his forehead. "Is that . . . ?"

"Birds," said Sarah. "It totally sounds like birds." She brushed by Marco and headed down the left-hand trail, toward the cacophony of sharp squawks and piercing whistles and singsong-ish tweets.

Marco called after her, "Hey, slow down! I think we should be careful."

But Sarah kept going, moving as fast as she could along the trail, dodging tree branches and pushing aside vines.

Marco was only a few steps behind her. "Sarah, wait! Please slow down!"

But Sarah didn't want to slow down. Her heart pounded, sure that her dad must have come the same way, heard the same noises she was hearing now. The path grew lighter, and she began to jog toward the opening, thinking that her dad could be just ahead, waiting for her and—

The ground suddenly disappeared from under her. She was falling.

Sarah screamed and clutched for a tree limb. Her hand scraped down the rough surface until it hit a notch. She reached up her other hand and clung to the branch, hanging there by outstretched arms, dangling over nothing but empty air. "Marco!' she screeched.

"Hang on!" Marco appeared on the edge of the cliff. His eyes were huge and his mouth hung open. His gaze went down, down, down, then snapped back up to her. "Whatever you do, do *not* look down."

Sarah twisted her head to the side and looked down. She screamed again.

"I told you not to look down!" yelled Marco.

Sarah was a few feet off the abrupt edge of a rocky cliff, with the closest ground more than fifty feet below. "Help!"

"Hang on," said Marco. He gingerly sidestepped to the edge, then got a grip on a thick tree branch with one hand as he reached out the other. "Just go hand over hand, see if you can move sideways."

Sarah scrunched her eyes shut. Her heart was pounding out of her chest as she panted, struggling to hang on. "I can't! I can't!"

"Sarah! Look at me."

His voice was so forceful that she had to do as he said. Marco held out his free hand as far as it would go, which was about three feet from Sarah. "You can do this. You only have to go this far, then I'll grab you, okay?"

She started to look down.

He yelled, "And quit looking down!"

Her gaze snapped back to him.

Marco nodded, his brown eyes huge. "That's it. Just keep looking at me." His face was red. He wiped some sweat off his forehead, then rubbed his hand on his shorts. "Okay, so just do what I tell you. Take your right hand and slide it over to your left hand."

"Okay." Sarah grunted as she slid her hand.

"Now slide your left hand over toward me as much as you can."

"It's on the notch!" Sarah said.

"You'll have to lift it a little."

Sarah held her breath, sure she would lose her grip. But her hand slid over the notch, toward the cliff and Marco and safety. She breathed out.

"Now slide your right hand over to the other one."

Sarah inched her way over, all the while feeling her arms and shoulders begin to burn. She had set the pull-up record for girls at her school, but hanging from a bar with a mat a few feet underneath was an entirely different thing from hanging off a cliff. The lower half of her body dangled, and she tried to hold it steady. "I can't hold on anymore."

"Yes you can! Sarah, look at me." Marco held out his hand.

Only a foot remained of the gap between them, and Sarah continued to painstakingly slide one hand, then the other. Tears blurred her vision. Unable to wipe them away, she felt them dripping down her face.

"That's it," said Marco. "You got this. Almost there!"

Sarah slid one more time and looked up.

Marco's hand was right there. "Okay, on three you're going to reach out your left hand to me as you try and push away with your right arm, okay?"

Sarah couldn't even nod, but managed to squeak out an okay.

"One," said Marco. "Two. Three!"

Sarah didn't move. She was frozen.

Marco let out a heavy breath. "You have to let go or it won't work."

"I'm scared!" she yelled.

"Either we do this now or you hang there until you get too tired to hold on."

"Fine!"

"Okay," said Marco. "On three. One. Two. Three!"

With a cry, Sarah pushed off with her right arm as she let go and reached out with her left. She felt the squeeze as Marco's hand clamped down on her wrist. Her right hand let go of the branch, and she was falling. She screamed, but then another strong hand joined the first around her left wrist, and she felt like her entire hand was being wrenched off as she hung by Marco's grip, her knees bumping against the side of the cliff.

"Climb!" he yelled.

She put her left foot on a slight protrusion in the cliff and felt herself rise a bit. She found another for her right foot, and then suddenly she was up, her head and shoulders above the edge of the cliff.

Marco had ahold of her wrist with both his hands, and his feet were propped against a tree trunk, leaning back as he held on to her. His face was contorted and he grunted as he tried to pull her up.

She bent a leg and got it over the edge, then let him pull her the rest of the way up. She landed facedown. Safe.

Sarah lay there for a moment, panting into the dirt. When she finally caught her breath, she lifted her head. Marco leaned back against the tree trunk, rubbing his hands.

"You okay?" she asked.

He nodded. "You?"

She sat up, then scooted farther away from the edge of the cliff. Her palms were red and scraped, as were her knees, but otherwise she seemed to be in one piece.

They sat in silence for a few minutes as she gently blew on her palms to help the stinging. She let out a deep breath and said, "I think you just saved my life."

He shrugged. "I figure I would have gotten in a lot of trouble if I'd let you fall off a cliff. Not exactly stepbrother of the year."

She grinned. "Well, thanks."

Suddenly, Marco's eyes narrowed and he pointed behind her.

She whirled in time to see a red bird fly in front of them, even with the edge of the cliff, so she could get a good look at it. Four wings. No beak. Mouth full of teeth. She gasped. "Your bird!"

Marco crawled over to the edge with her and they lay shoulder to shoulder on their bellies, heads at the cliff's edge, staring downward.

Sarah sucked in a breath, unable to speak as she took in the sights and sounds coming up from the open valley below.

Marco asked exactly what she was thinking, "Where in the world are we?"

12

Marco was still breathing hard from his rescue of Sarah; his heart raced, maybe from the exertion, or maybe from what he saw from their perch high on the cliff.

A green valley spread below them, bordered on three sides by steep, rocky walls. The far end, about half a mile away, seemed to narrow and open onto the beach, but Marco couldn't tell for sure. Down deep, he wasn't sure if any of what he was seeing was even real.

Creatures filled the valley—birds and animals—but types he'd never seen *anywhere*. He watched a red bird like the one he'd seen fly past. A smaller, purple one buzzed like a bee as it swooped up and over them, coming close and hovering just a foot in front of them. Instead of feathers, the bird's tail end brandished a yellow-and-black-striped stinger.

"I hate bees!" Sarah scrambled up on her knees.

"Stay still," whispered Marco.

Sarah froze.

The bird buzzed closer, until it was inches from Sarah's face. Sarah sucked in a breath and scrunched her eyes shut. The bird darted to the side a few feet, then back in front of Sarah.

Marco wondered whether he should try and shoo it away. But then he took another look at the stinger and just crossed his fingers that it would leave on its own. After a few more seconds, the thing seemed to lose interest and flew away, probably in search of something better.

"It's gone," said Marco.

Sarah blew out the breath she'd been holding. "Did you see that bird? It had a stinger!"

"I know," said Marco.

"Look!" Sarah pointed across the valley. Smugly, she said, "My kangaroo."

Marco watched as the kangaroo hopped, the large lion's paws not seeming to slow it down. "Whoa." His gaze drifted to another animal not far from it. With thick gray skin like armor and a blocky, muscular rear end, it resembled a rhino from the back. "A rhino!"

Then the creature turned to the side and revealed its profile.

"Not a rhino," said Sarah.

Instead of a horn on its snout, the horn came out of its forehead.

"It's like a . . . a . . . rhino*corn,*" said Sarah.

Marco whispered, "How is that possible?"

"How is that bird with the stinger possible? Or that kangaroo?" Sarah said. "This is like the Island of Misfit Toys. Only they're animals."

"I wish Nacho could see this," said Marco.

"He would probably know the answer to all of this," said Sarah.

Marco grinned at her. "Probably." He turned back to watch the rhinocorn graze. "There must be a way down there. If that was what ran past us on the path, there must be a fast way down there."

As they watched, a large black cat with an odd tuft of scarlet hair on its chin lowered itself to the ground behind a large rock. The feline's red tail began swishing as it stared at a squirrel with a beaver's tail. "Some of those things look hungry," said Sarah. "I do not want to go down there."

Marco gestured into the open space in front of them. "Well, we can't go any farther this way."

Sarah said, "Let's go back to the V in the path and take the other way."

"Okay," said Marco. He hoped they would find a way to get down to the valley. He wasn't sure what would happen once they got there, but he felt that it might put them closer to finding his brother and Sarah's dad.

"But I'm not going down there. I mean, if the path looks like it starts leading toward those *things,* I'm not going." Sarah looked like she was about to cry again.

Marco nodded. Reluctantly, he left his perch and followed Sarah back down the path. After being in the bright sun at the edge of the cliff, Marco found the light under the cover of the trees especially dim. He looked around, wary for any other creatures that may have found their way into the trees.

Sarah asked, "Do you think those animals have something to do with the Curator?"

"Maybe," replied Marco. But he hoped they would not find out the answer anytime soon. They reached the V. "This is it," said Marco. He rubbed his cheek on his shoulder to soak up some of the sweat on his face. He took a long, lingering look at the path they'd taken from their camp.

Sarah followed his gaze and said, "We *could* go back to the beach. Maybe they made it back and are wondering where we are." She sounded more optimistic than he felt. "Dad's probably mad that we came looking for him."

Marco pulled a bottle of water out of the canvas bag and handed it to Sarah, then pulled out another. Without thinking, he put the bottle to his face, hoping to cool off; he was disappointed to find the plastic just as hot as he was. Would he ever drink cold water again? He unscrewed the top and took a long, unpleasantly warm swig. At least it was wet. He stuffed the bottle back in the bag. "Ready?"

Sarah nodded. "You first."

That path looked much the same as the first, except that they seemed to be descending the entire time. The area grew lighter more quickly than it had on the other path. Soon, they emerged from the trees, facing a rock wall that rose about fifty feet above them.

Sarah tipped her head back and gazed up. "Is this the same one I fell off?"

Marco crossed his arms and looked around. "This might be the end of that valley. At least, the opposite side of where it ends." He turned all the way around and let his hands drop with a slap onto his thighs. "I'm confused now."

"We're lost?" asked Sarah.

"No, we can always go back on the path. I'm just trying to figure out how to go farther this way." A pile of boulders lay there, covered with vines. He walked over to them and started to climb.

"Seriously?" Sarah put her hands on her hips. "Because we haven't had enough cliffs for one day?"

Marco looked over his shoulder at her. "I'm just going

up a bit, to see if I can see something." He grabbed at the vine on the top boulder for a handhold and it snapped.

"Whoa!" He fell back onto his butt and slid down the boulders, landing on the ground with a jolt. He winced and put a hand on his back, which stung from being scraped. "Ow."

"Marco." Sarah sounded funny.

"I'm fine," he said. "Thanks for asking." He stood up and brushed himself off. But Sarah hadn't moved. She stood there, gawking at something behind him.

He turned. By tearing off the vine, he'd uncovered the boulder. Two identical circular indentations about the size and shape of doughnuts sat across from each other above the top of a jutting portion of stone. Beneath that a crescent curled up into a smile.

"It's a face," said Marco.

"A face rock." Sarah pointed at it. When Marco didn't say anything, she repeated, "A *face rock*. What Cash said Fox was searching for!"

Marco put a hand over his mouth for a moment. Impossible. Fox had seen the island and had discounted it, ruled it out as the one he'd been marooned on. "But Cash said that Fox had taken one look and said it couldn't be the island, that there had barely been any trees on it."

Sarah glanced sideways at where they'd come out of. "But this island is jammed with trees."

"Yeah, *now,*" said Marco. "Maybe they weren't here when he was."

Sarah shook her head, "I'm no expert, but I know trees don't grow that fast. And don't you think Fox would have mentioned the rhinocorn or the bird with a stinger on its tail? Or the Curator?"

Marco said, "But how do you explain it?"

"I don't think any of this was here when Fox was marooned. I think all of this—*happened*—since he left." She paused for a moment. "And in that time, at some point, Captain Norm came here and found that trunk."

Marco nodded. "But it still doesn't explain how all this ended up here."

"I know," said Sarah. "Which is why we need to find the answer."

Marco shook his head. "Oh, no way. We are out here to look for your dad and my brother. We're not here to look for something we may not want to find."

Sarah swallowed. "But what if my dad isn't okay? What if he got taken just like Cash did?"

"So you believe her story now?" he asked.

She shrugged. "I don't know. With everything we've seen, how can we not believe her?"

Marco nodded. "I know. But your dad is okay. Ahab was with him. He wouldn't have let anything happen to him."

Sarah said, "Marco. Nacho doesn't have Ahab. He's alone. Just like Cash was."

Marco felt his heartbeat speed up. What if Nacho was in trouble? And what if Cash had been telling the truth? And what if the same thing that happened to her was going to happen to his little brother?

Sarah looked over at the rocks. "Do you think that's the way to where Cash got taken?"

Marco stared at the rocks. If there was any possibility that his brother had been taken, he was going to find him. Marco sighed. "I have no idea. But it's worth a try."

13

Sarah began to climb, avoiding the vines in order not to duplicate Marco's mistake. But to keep her balance, she had to set her scraped hands on the boulders, which made them sting even more than they already did. She tried her best to ignore the discomfort as she kept climbing. When she reached the top of the stack of boulders, she stuck her face into a foot-wide crevice. Light came through from the other side, about fifty yards away. "There's a passageway here!"

"But Cash didn't say anything about that," Marco called from below.

Sarah leaned back and looked down at him. "But she didn't know how she got to the Curator's cave, remember? She went into the trees and the net fell on her, and the next thing she remembered, she was waking up in her cell. She doesn't know how she got there. And neither do we." For a moment she studied the crevice, thinking there was no way anyone could have hauled Cash through there. Sarah was not a fan of enclosed spaces, and this space looked far too tight for her.

"I'm not even sure we can squeeze through here." She turned sideways and reached out an arm into the crevice, then took a step. The walls were close, only inches away from her on either side. "Nope." She stepped back out and called down to Marco, "It's too skinny, I think."

Marco held up his hand. "Well, now what?"

Just as Sarah started to climb back down, the ground rumbled beneath them. From her high vantage point, Sarah saw gray flashes through the trees as a creature ran by. She pointed. "The rhinocorn—it's back! Hurry!"

Marco scrambled up the boulders. "Go!" he yelled.

Sarah's heart pounded. "Into the crack?"

"We don't have a choice!"

Sarah turned sideways and slid into the crevice, hoping that the walls wouldn't get any closer together. "Marco?"

"Made it!" said Marco, breathing hard. "This is tight."

Sarah felt his hand brush her shoulder and sighed with relief. She tried to turn her head, but smacked it against the hard wall. There was no longer enough room to turn her head around to look at him. Her heart began to pound harder, and her breaths became shorter and quicker. "Marco?" Her voice shook.

His voice had a forced calm to it, far more cheery than usual. "Just keep going. Slow and steady. We've got this."

"Okay." She slid one foot to meet the next, slid the other one out, and then repeated the actions, slowly closing the gap to the other end of the crack in the rock. The space continued to tighten, the walls closing in. A scream bubbled up and she swallowed it. Instead, she shouted, "I want to go back! I want to go back!"

"I don't think I can," said Marco.

"What do you mean?" Sarah cried.

"Well, for one, the rhinocorn is probably waiting out there for us."

"And that's it?" Sarah asked. "Maybe it left already."

"Um, not the only reason. I don't think I can go back," he said. "Please, you've got to keep going."

Sarah shut her eyes and took a deep breath. *You can do this. You have to do this to find Dad.* She opened her eyes and focused on the light, less than twenty yards away. Her feet scuffed as they slid and she heard Marco do the same behind her.

"That's it," he said. "We've got this."

One step at a time, one shallow breath at a time,

Sarah made her way closer and closer to the end of the crevice, the seam of light growing bigger with each moment. With only a few feet to go, the passage narrowed so that the walls scraped against her back and front. She swallowed down a scream. And then, with one last step, her lead arm was free, out in the air, followed by her head and one leg, then the other, and finally her other arm.

She took a few steps into freedom, then doubled over, hands on her knees, and blew out a breath.

"A little help?"

She lifted her head.

An arm waved at her from the opening. "I think I'm kinda stuck."

Sarah walked over to him. Marco's face was sideways, his body crunched between the two walls. She took ahold of his arm and yanked.

"Ow!" Marco grimaced.

Sarah dropped his arm. "Sorry."

"No, don't stop. You have to pull." Again, he held his arm out to her. "I'll suck in as much as I can."

She widened her stance, gripped his arm, and pulled with everything she had. She felt him move slightly toward her, so she took half a step back with one foot and pulled again. Something gave, and suddenly she fell backward onto her butt.

Marco landed right next to her, facedown. "Oomph!"

"You okay?" she asked.

He lifted his head up. His cheeks and chin bore several scrapes. "Yeah, thanks. Better than being stuck in there."

Sarah nodded and looked back at the crevice. "I just thought of something."

"What?" asked Marco.

"There's no way my dad would have fit through there. Or Ahab. I was so worried about wondering how Cash got to the Curator that I didn't stop to think about who we're really looking for." She sighed.

"I was going to say something, but . . ." Marco stopped.

Sarah raised an eyebrow. "But what?"

"I just have a gut feeling. I feel like . . ."

"What?" whispered Sarah.

"Cash's story is real. Everything about it. And I feel like Nacho or your dad . . . that they are already there. With the Curator. And we have to get there however we can." He lifted and lowered a shoulder.

"It's not like we had a choice." Sarah sighed. "It's too late now. We can't go back through there. But where do we go now?"

"I think, maybe . . ." Marco pointed. "There."

Sarah twisted her upper body around. A path curved around another set of boulders, disappearing after about thirty yards. "Is that it?"

"Only one way to find out." The canvas bag had fallen off his arm when he fell, so he picked it up as he got to his feet. Marco held out a hand to Sarah and she took it, letting him pull her to her feet.

She brushed herself off and followed her stepbrother.

14

The path led them into the trees. They kept walking. Marco was so tired of looking at trees that he just focused on the ground as he walked, avoiding roots and vines.

Sarah gasped.

Marco stopped and turned around.

Her eyes were trained over his head, and he slowly leaned his head back and followed her gaze. A tree branch stretched out straight above them. Ripe orange fruit dangled from it, and Marco reached up and plucked one. The shape was that of an orange, but instead of a dimpled peel, it had a shiny skin. He held it up to his nose. "Smells like an orange."

"Don't eat it!" said Sarah.

"I think it's okay." With a crunch, Marco took a small bite and chewed. The texture of an apple with the taste of an orange. Odd, but not bad. Kind of fun. He reached up and plucked one for Sarah. "Try it."

Sarah scrunched up her nose, but took a small, tentative bite. Her eyes lit up. "That's kinda good." She took a bigger bite.

Marco reached up and picked a few, then put them in the bag. They kept going for about a hundred yards, where the path led them back onto the beach. Marco stopped to look back the way they had come.

"Are you kidding? We could have stayed on the beach and ended up here." Sarah sounded frustrated.

Marco checked the angle of the shoreline compared with where they had gone through the woods. "I don't think so." He smiled. "Actually, I think we stumbled on the shortcut."

"But Cash said she ran out of the cave right to the beach," said Sarah.

Marco said. "I know. But that may have been the long way. Like going around the outside of a circle. We cut off part of that circle." He looked at Sarah. "So, yeah, I think we maybe could have gotten here from the beach, but it would have taken us longer."

Sarah's eyes widened. "So if my dad and Ahab stayed on the beach—"

"And my brother," added Marco.

"They could still be walking! Maybe we can still

catch them." Sarah began running down the beach. She stopped and waved her arm at him. "Come on!"

Marco firmed up his grip on the canvas bag and ran after her. He hoped she was right, that they would run into John and Nacho before they encountered the Curator. Because then he and John could go on, find the person Cash told them about, solve the mystery.

Or—what sounded like a better option to him at the moment—they could all just go back to the beach and hope that Cash's grandpa showed up to rescue them before the Curator came looking . . .

Sarah was quicker in the thick sand, so Marco moved down to the harder-packed layer so he could catch up a bit. He happened to look down and stopped running. "Sarah!" he yelled.

She slowed and turned around, walking backward. "What?"

He pointed down. "Footprints." He set his foot next to one of the deeply imprinted tracks not yet washed away. His foot was bigger. "They're my brother's!"

Sarah jogged toward him, panting. "What about my dad? Or the dog?"

Marco shook his head. "The tide is already washing some of these away, and they would have been here before him . . ."

"So they're gone," said Sarah. "If they were even here." She wiped away a tear that Marco hadn't noticed fall. She looked up at him with watery eyes.

"They were here," he said. "I know they were."

"How do you know?" Sarah sniffled. "We have no way of knowing." She glared out at the lagoon.

Marco hesitated, then reached out and put a hand on her shoulder.

She glanced sideways at it, then up at him.

"We'll find them. All of them. My brother. Your dad. The dog. We will." He swallowed. "I promise."

Sarah gave the slightest of nods, then swiped a hand across her eyes and turned away. "Let's go then." She started walking again.

Marco took a last glance at his brother's footprints and followed Sarah up into the soft sand. They walked in silence for close to a half hour, trudging through the sand as the hot sun beat down on them. They stopped to get a drink and Marco looked at the lagoon longingly.

Sarah watched him as she took a warm sip from the plastic bottle.

He pulled the collar of his drenched T-shirt away from his skin. "I'm sweating to death. Worse than this morning." He asked, "Think we could jump in, just to cool off?"

Sarah's bangs were matted to her forehead and her face was red and sweaty. "But we need to find them."

"I know, but just like five minutes. It would reenergize us so we could move faster." Marco raised his eyebrows. "Please?"

She nodded. "Okay. But I'm not getting salt water in my clean hair."

They went down to the water. Sarah sat down to remove her shoes. Marco kicked his off, peeled off his socks and stuffed them in his shoes, then pulled his T-shirt over his head and tossed it by the canvas bag. Running into the waves, he dove, surfacing a few yards farther out. His wet hair clung to his face as he turned to face the beach. He flipped it out of his eyes. "It feels as good as the waterfall pool! Woo!" He went under again, then popped up, bobbing there.

Wading in, Sarah seemed content to get wet up to her shorts. She leaned over to cup some water and toss it onto her face. She grinned.

Marco figured they would regret this later. The salt would dry on their skin and feel crusty and unpleasant, but he was too hot to care. Maybe they could go back and swim at the waterfall when they'd found everyone. Maybe his mom would even feel better and want to go.

Sarah jumped as a wave came in, then laughed. She started to wave at Marco, but her arm stopped midair.

The smile dropped off her face, replaced by an open mouth and wide eyes.

Sarah pointed beyond Marco and screamed.

Marco didn't even look to see what it was; he just assumed something bad. He began a rapid overhand crawl, as fast as he could, trying to ignore his pounding heart and trembling limbs.

"Marco!" Sarah kept screaming his name.

Marco didn't stop kicking and stroking until his knees brushed the sand. He stood and plowed through the waves until he could run, then tripped and fell in a heap at Sarah's feet.

He rolled onto his back, panting, and looked up at her.

Sarah said, "Shark."

He shuddered. That's what he'd been afraid of. He lay back and shut his eyes, panting, relieved to be out of the water. He was definitely only swimming at the waterfall from now on.

"Marco."

He opened his eyes and gazed up at Sarah. She still seemed frozen.

"What?" he asked. "I made it. I'm fine."

She shook her head and pointed at the lagoon. "Something isn't right."

Marco sat up. About ten yards offshore, a dorsal fin paced back and forth. "He's so slow."

Sarah nodded. "And that's a really big fin."

Marco got to his feet. "That's too shallow there. How is he even swimming—"

As if the beast had heard them, the fin stopped moving parallel to the shore and turned. Then it stopped completely, not moving at all.

"That's not possible," whispered Sarah.

Marco said nothing; he simply watched.

The fin began moving again, inching toward the beach, heading straight toward them.

Marco's hands trembled. "That's way too shallow." He started to back up and Sarah stayed with him. She grabbed their shoes and Marco's shirt and stuffed them in the bag, then hooked her arm through the handle. "There's no way that—"

The fin came closer to shore, rising higher as the water grew shallower. Silvery gray flesh appeared, until the shark's monstrous pointy, cone-shaped snout emerged, dripping; the black beady eyes on each side stared, unblinking.

"It's a great white," whispered Marco. He didn't think there were supposed to be great whites in the South Pacific.

"What is it doing?" yelled Sarah.

Marco shook his head, but took a few steps back,

his heart pounding faster now than when he'd been swimming.

The shark's gigantic mouth dropped open, revealing rows of white triangular razor teeth set in a cushion of red.

Sarah shrieked. "Why isn't it stopping?"

The shark advanced toward them, until the gills appeared and then the pectoral fins; its entire front half was almost all the way out of the water, the waves continuing to ebb and flow as the creature crept closer to shore.

And to them.

"How's it doing that?" asked Sarah in a shaky voice.

Marco gasped. He grabbed Sarah's arm and pulled her back as he pointed at the bottom of the shark. "That's how!"

The shiny silver skin on the sides of the shark gave way to dull yellow-and-black-scaled reptilian legs that protruded from the bottom of the creature. Each foot had five toes, each embedded with a sharp claw.

As if to demonstrate how those powerful-looking legs and feet worked, the shark surged toward them.

"Run!" yelled Marco. They turned and sprinted up the beach.

Marco glanced back over his shoulder as he ran.

Shocked at how quickly the heavy creature moved on those small but agile feet, Marco put on a burst of speed before facing all the way forward. His legs tangled and he sprawled on the ground, smacking his right knee on a rock. Wincing, he sat up.

Sarah screamed.

The creature scuttled toward him.

All he could see was that bloody-red maw—and those white jagged teeth—mere yards away and closing.

Sarah seemed frozen.

"Run!" yelled Marco. He scrambled to his feet and began to back up, limping, looking around for a weapon. He picked up a rock, ready to throw. His heart pounded as his mouth dried up.

No stupid rock was going to keep that thing from eating him. Still, with both hands he raised it above his head, ready to heave it—a last-chance shot of desperation.

But the creature paused.

"Look," said Sarah. "The gills!"

On either side of its head, the gills trembled, almost flapping.

"It can't breathe!" said Marco. "It has to go back in the water." He hoped he was right, and even crossed his fingers as he kept backing up.

Slowly, the creature—massive mouth still open—retreated toward the water, turning to move headfirst into the waves. There, the fin inching into the water, it slowly disappeared.

Marco dropped the rock, which landed with a thud.

"Are you okay?" asked Sarah.

"Yeah." He leaned over, head down, resting his hands on his knees. "I need a sec."

Sarah came up beside him. "I thought you were . . ." She didn't finish.

Marco figured he knew what she was thinking. That he had been about to become fish food. He turned his head and looked up at her. "Yeah. Me too." He straightened back up and blew out a deep breath.

"That, that . . . shark*odile*." Sarah's voice was low and solemn as she stared down at the ground. "It can't have been real."

"Any more than the rhinocorn. Or those birds, or . . ." He shook his head.

Sarah stood up and gasped. "Look!"

Marco whirled around, expecting some new and dangerous creature.

Instead, the mouth of a cave yawned, dark and bleak in the bright sunlight. Was it the one they'd been looking for? The one Cash escaped from?

Despite the sweat still drying on his body, Marco shivered.

15

Sarah watched Marco limp toward the cave. She pulled on his arm to stop him. "Are you sure you're okay?"

He nodded. "Hurt my knee." He flexed it a couple of times. "Not that bad. Only bruised, I think."

She held up the bag. "We should put our shoes back on."

Marco also donned his shirt. When they were ready, Sarah said, "Well, I'll go first." She walked ahead of Marco and stepped into the cave. For the tiniest of moments as she passed through the mouth, a shock—more like a ripple—ran through her body. She gasped, but before she could say anything, or warn Marco, he was right behind her.

His eyes widened and his mouth dropped open.

"Did you feel that?" Sarah asked.

Marco nodded. He looked past Sarah, deeper into the blackness that lay ahead of them.

Sarah reached into the bag for the flashlight, but jerked back at the touch of something ice cold. "What in the—" She reached in the bag again and pulled out the water bottle. The cold of it burned her hand and she dropped it, where it rolled next to Marco's foot. He nudged it with his toe and the bottle rolled, no water sloshing inside.

Sarah crouched beside it. "It's ice. The water is ice."

"That's impossible," said Marco. But he leaned over to touch the bottle. The water in the bottle was solid ice. "But it was warm. Not even half an hour ago it was *warm*."

Sarah said, "I'm getting out of here. Come on." She turned to walk out, but suddenly a blue film covered the mouth of the cave and sent her flying backward, screaming. She landed on her back, and her head bounced off the floor of the cave.

Marco knelt beside her. "Are you hurt?"

Sarah scrunched up her face and put a hand at the back of her head. "I don't think so. What was that?"

Marco turned to look at the mouth of the cave, clear once again. He stood up.

"Don't try it!" called Sarah.

"I won't," said Marco. With his foot, he rolled the water bottle to position it. Then he gave it a hard swipe with the side of his foot, sending it careening toward the mouth of the cave.

Instantly, the space turned blue and the water bottle exploded, sending shards of cold plastic and ice everywhere. Sarah shrieked as they both put up their hands to shield their faces.

When it stopped, Marco lowered his arms and looked at Sarah. "Well, I guess we're not going out that way." He looked at the dark passageway looming ahead. "Ready?"

She got to her feet, still rubbing her head. "Do I have a choice?"

Marco shook his head.

She took the flashlight and walked just in front of Marco. She had to admit, she was happy he was with her. He seemed almost protective of her since he'd saved her on the cliff. And she didn't know what she'd have done if he'd gotten eaten up on the beach. She was beginning to feel like she could trust him. And, to be honest, she liked him as much as she liked Nacho. As stepbrothers went, they weren't all that bad.

The rock ceiling was only a few feet above their heads. Sarah stretched her arms out to the side, and there were barely a few inches to spare. She sighed.

"Better than the last time," said Marco.

"*Oh* yeah," said Sarah. She was relieved that this time,

instead of everything closing in as they moved forward, the ceiling gradually drifted higher, until it was way over their heads. The walls widened, expanding enough so that they could walk side by side.

Sarah realized that the blackness of the cave had lightened considerably. She stopped walking and flicked off the flashlight. Although the way in front of them was dim, they could still see. She flicked the flashlight back on. "Why is it so light?" she asked.

Marco pointed ahead of them. "It gets even lighter up there."

A few more yards, and Sarah shut off the flashlight and stowed it in the bag. Marco stepped forward and the place suddenly brightened, so much that it seemed like they were outside in the sun.

Sarah tilted her head back and gasped. The ceiling seemed like it was miles overhead. The sides and straight in front of them were lit only a few yards in, so she couldn't tell how big the space was.

Marco took a step forward.

Snap! Snap! Snap!

The noises continued as lights flipped on, bank by bank, illuminating the space beyond.

Sarah took in the sight in front of them. Not believing at first, she shut her eyes, and then opened them again.

"Whoa."

They stood in a cavern so humongous she couldn't even see the end.

"This thing must be like six or seven soccer fields long," said Marco. "Longer maybe."

"What are those?" asked Sarah.

Rows of white modules lined both sides of the cavern. Their fronts made of glass, but too frosty to see inside. She stood in front of the closest one, which only reached as high as her waist. She turned her head and looked down the rows, where the modules gradually grew bigger and wider, some as tall as houses. She focused on the one in front of her and set a hand on the glass. "Ow!" She snatched it back.

Marco touched it lightly with his fingertips. "Cold," he said. But he set his hand on the frost, holding it there a moment. When he took it away, a little of the frost had melted. He did it again, until he had a clear patch the size of a dollar bill. He leaned down.

"Careful!" said Sarah.

"I'm just taking a look," he said. He peered inside, then stood back up. "It's a goat."

"It's a what?" asked Sarah.

Marco shrugged. "A goat. A billy goat."

"Let me see." Sarah held her face up to the clear patch of glass. A white billy goat, with a great scruff of a beard, stood motionless inside. But as she watched, his chest moved slightly and the tiniest bit of steam came out his nostrils.

She stood back up. "He's frozen."

Sarah looked on the front of the nodule.

"What are you looking for?" asked Marco.

"A handle. Or something to open it." Sarah ran her hands down the front of the frost-covered nodule and felt some lumps. She blew on the frost, which wasn't as heavy as that on the glass, and it melted fairly quickly. "Look!"

A keypad about the size of a cell phone, with symbols, lay about halfway down the side of the nodule. Sarah reached out to touch one, but Marco grabbed her wrist. "Hey! I don't think you should do that."

She shot him a defiant look, but realized he was right. "I won't." Her eyes narrowed. "Hey, I've seen these letters before. Or symbols, whatever they are."

Marco leaned in to see them better. "Yeah. Where have I . . . " His eyes widened and he turned to meet Sarah's gaze. "The symbols. They're the same ones."

"The same ones what?" asked Sarah.

"The same ones that are on the trunk," said Marco. "The mermaid trunk."

16

Marco peered in disbelief at the symbols, the same ones that curved around the top of the trunk that he'd dragged off the ruined HMS *Moonflight.* He scratched his head. "I don't get it." He asked Sarah, "They're the same, right? I'm not just imagining things?"

Sarah squinted at the module. "Yeah. I think so." She frowned. "But how could they be the same as the ones on the trunk Fox brought to the island?"

Marco thought about it for a moment. "Maybe we assumed that he'd brought it here. But what if he didn't? What if he found it here when he was marooned, left with the plan of coming back for it, but then Captain Norm came and found it?"

"But he came from Africa. It sounded like he got it there." She frowned. "But how can it be the same?" asked

Sarah. "The same people who did all this"—she spread out her arms—"made the trunk too?"

"I don't know." Marco shook his head as he stood back up. He wasn't sure they were even talking about people anymore. None of it seemed natural. None of it seemed like it belonged on this planet. It all seemed way more like it was *not of this Earth*.

He shivered as he stepped to the next module. There, he held his palms on the frost glass as long as he could, then blew on them to warm up before setting them there again. A small, misshapen circle cleared and he looked through it. A white goat stood there, motionless like the first. "Another goat." He took a longer look. There was no beard or horns. "This one's female, I think."

"Let me see." Sarah bent to see in, and then straightened back up. "But they're normal, right? Like no extra horns or wings or weird feet or anything?"

Marco looked into the first module again. "No, they seem like normal goats." He took a step back and shook his head. Why was there an island full of weird animals, and then a cave with normal ones? He couldn't make any sense of it.

Sarah strode down the row of modules, like she was looking for something. Finally, she stopped at one that was taller than their house back in California. The glass front stretched up about ten feet, but she set a hand on the frost at eye level. Marco caught up with her and set a hand on it too. A few moments later, they had a patch about the size of an envelope. Sarah leaned forward.

"What do you see?" asked Marco.

"Weird." She didn't say anything for a moment, and then she stepped back. Sarah scrunched up her nose and shrugged. "They're like . . . gray tree trunks or something. I can't tell."

Marco stepped close to the glass, so near that his breath fogged it up. Inside the module he saw two thick, gray trees. At least, that's what they looked like. He was taller than Sarah, and stood up on his tiptoes and looked down. Four semicircles of a slightly different color were embedded on the front of the bottom of the gray things.

Marco sucked in. Not just semicircles. They were . . . toenails. "Whoa." He stepped back. "Not trees."

"What?" asked Sarah.

Marco said, "I'm pretty sure those aren't trees." He reached up as high as he could and placed his hands there until he couldn't stand the cold, then did it again until he had a clear spot. He knelt down. "Here, get up on my shoulders."

"Why?" Sarah made a face.

He pointed up. "To get a better look."

She set the bag down. "Fine." Sarah pushed on his shoulders. "Lower."

Marco sunk down more, even though it hurt his injured knee.

Sarah swung a leg over each shoulder. "I'm gonna fall!" She put her hands on the module to steady herself.

"Going up." Marco stood. "Can you see?"

"To the left a little!"

Marco tried to move, but lost his balance and tipped to the left.

Sarah squealed. "Watch it!"

Marco righted himself, then leaned forward so he could put his hands on the cold module to keep his balance.

"Okay, that's good." Sarah leaned closer to the glass. "Oh, whoa."

"What?" asked Marco. The strain on his legs wasn't bad because his stepsister wasn't very heavy, but his hands burned from the cold glass.

"It's an elephant. With tusks. Frozen, like the goats." She rapped her knuckles on the top of his head. "Let me down."

"Gladly." Marco squatted and held up his hands.

She grasped them. "On three. One, two, three!"

He pushed up and she vaulted over his head to the floor. He straightened up and flexed his knee a couple times. "Seriously? An elephant?"

She nodded, then added, "A normal one. No extra parts."

"Wow," said Marco. He tilted his head at the next module, which was identical in size and shape. "You think that one's a female?"

Sarah nodded. "Yeah." She narrowed her eyes. "Is this some kind of Noah's Ark?" She looked down the rows. "You think there's two of everything frozen in here?"

"Maybe." Marco shivered. His shirt was still damp with sweat, and he was getting chilled more and more as they stayed there. "And we're going to be the next two frozen if we don't find a way out of here."

"Okay," said Sarah. She scooped up the bag. "But can we look in one more?"

Marco nodded. "Pick a shorter one though." He started doing jumping jacks, trying to warm up as Sarah ran across the cavern to the other row of modules. She picked one that was only a few feet taller than she was and stuck her hand on the frost. Marco joined her as she pulled off her hand and looked in. "Oh."

"Lemme see." Marco waited until Sarah moved, then looked in. A black-and-white cow, small rivulets of steam coming out of its large, shiny pink nostrils. "A Holstein." He glanced at the module next to it and raised his eyebrows. "My guess is there's a bull in that one."

"I'll see," said Sarah. She blew on her hands, then placed them on the frost, clearing a spot. She leaned in. "Yeah, I'd say so. Huge horns."

Marco said, "So some are domestic animals and some are wild."

"This is so weird." Sarah hugged herself, her arms covered with goose bumps. "I want to find my dad."

Marco nodded. He wanted to find his brother, if he was there, and then get out. He shivered again, then pointed. "Let's follow the rows. They have to end at some point, right?"

"Yeah." Sarah reached out and touched the frost-covered keypad with symbols. Then she leaned over and looked at the one on the module next to it. "They're different."

"Different how?" asked Marco.

Sarah compared them again. "I think they're the names of the animals. But in whatever weird language it is." She met his gaze. "It's like . . . the module was made for the animal. With the animal's name on it. *Before the animal was ever in it.*"

Marco frowned. "As if the modules are for—"

They both uttered the word at the same time:

"Collecting."

A collection.

Marco turned and looked around the cavern at all the modules.

They were standing in the midst of someone's *collection.* And they needed to get out *before they became part of it.*

17

Sarah started shaking. She didn't know whether it was from the cold or from fear, but she couldn't stand still. "Let's go." She grabbed Marco's arm and started jogging toward the end of the row. They had gone about a hundred yards when Marco came to a halt in front of a module.

"Look," he said. The module's glass was clear. "It's empty."

Sarah ran her fingertips over the keypad. "I wonder what is meant to be in here."

"I don't want to know," said Marco. "Let's keep going."

They walked fast, past more empty modules, until they were nearly at the end. Sarah asked, "It's a wall! What do we do when we—" She stopped when she saw Marco.

He was in front of a module that came up to his chest. The glass in front of it was just beginning to frost over, and only a few white stars had formed on it. His mouth hung open as he stepped closer.

"Marco?" When he didn't answer her, Sarah said, "You're scaring me! Say something."

Marco simply placed his palm on the glass, riveted by whatever lay inside.

"Marco?" Sarah joined him and gazed inside the module.

The black fur was the first thing she saw, but then her eyes were drawn right to the silver anchor-shaped tag.

AHABB.

She slapped her hand over her mouth before she could scream. "Oh no. No. No. No." She dropped her hand and turned to Marco, his eyes wide. She turned back to the module. There was the slightest tinge of frost on the end of Ahab's nose, where a trickle of steam came out. His brown eyes stared straight ahead, looking at nothing. "Oh no." Sarah's eyes filled with tears. She set her hand on the glass. "I'll get you out of there. I promise."

Marco said, "Your dad has to be here. We have to find him."

Sarah sniffled and wiped her nose. "Here?" And then she realized what he meant. Her heart pounded as a rush of heat ran up her neck and face; a tremor started in her hands that had nothing to do with the cold. "Frozen?"

Marco started to say, "No, I didn't mean . . . " But he stopped, and bit his lower lip. "I don't know."

"No!" She backed away from him. "He can't be." She backed into a nearby module, which was about the height of her shoulders, and whirled around. It was empty. She went to the next one, which was slightly shorter. Also empty. The next module was about six and a half feet tall. The frost was just beginning to gather on the glass and she stopped and looked inside.

Her eyes traveled up the tan legs and the khaki shorts and the polo shirt, stopping when they reached the glasses, fogged so that she couldn't see her father's eyes. She screamed and pounded on the glass. "Noooooooo!"

"Sarah!" Marco tried to grab her arm, but she flailed out and shoved him away. She went back to the module, catching the keypad in her gaze. She started pushing on the symbols, then began smacking them with the flat of her hand. "I'll get you out! I'll get you out!" Tears rolled down her cheeks as sobs caught in her throat. "I'll get you out!"

"Sarah!"

She ignored him, and kept pounding on the keypad until her hands felt bruised. She fell to her knees and lay her forehead against the glass, staring at her father. "I'll get you out."

Marco uttered something in Spanish.

Sarah moved just enough so she could look sideways at him. He stood motionless in front of the neighboring module, his fists squeezing and then releasing. He repeated whatever he had said, then hit the glass with the side of his fist.

Sarah got to her feet and went to stand next to him.

Nacho was in that module, standing in his khaki shorts and purple Eco-Scout shirt and black flip-flops. A small cloud of vapor came out of his nostrils, and his dark eyes fixed on something beyond them as his hair stuck up a little on top.

Sarah put a hand on Marco's arm. He set a hand on it. "We'll get them out." His voice was low and deep, almost a growl. "We'll find whoever did this."

WHOOOOOSSSSHHHH!

At the sound overhead, Sarah snapped her head back, just in time to see a net falling on top of her.

18

Marco also saw the net, and shoved Sarah away from it. Instead of falling right on top of her, it just caught one of her legs, but stuck tight as she tried to kick it off. "Don't touch it!" yelled Marco. "It'll stick to anything."

"There's a knife in the bag," said Sarah.

Marco dug through and found it, then started trying to cut through the net. But as soon as the knife touched the net, it stuck to it. "Oh no." He looked at Sarah. "I don't know what—"

Suddenly, her eyes bulged and she pointed behind him. "The Curator!"

Marco whirled around.

A bald man in a blue jumpsuit, slightly shorter than Marco, held up a white tube and pointed it at him. With a *WHOOOSSSHHH,* a white net shot out.

Marco managed to dodge it, then ran toward the man. Just as another net was propelled out of the tube, Marco flew up with a kick and knocked the thing out of the man's hands, the net floating harmlessly to the ground. He then kicked again, straight into the man's chest, knocking him flat on the ground.

"Be careful!" Sarah yelled.

Marco leapt onto the man, straddling him as he put his hands around his throat. "Let them go! You've got to let them go!"

Marco's hand's tightened, and the man's green eyes widened as he reached up with his wrinkled, age-spotted hands and grasped Marco's forearms. There wasn't a lot of strength there, and Marco had no problem holding him down. "Tell me how to get the net off! Tell me how to open those things!"

The bald man squeezed his eyes shut and rocked his head from side to side.

Then, suddenly, red stubble appeared all over the man's head. Marco watched in amazement as auburn hair sprouted from the man's head, flowing soft and shiny, not stopping until it reached Marco's arms. "What the—" His gaze went back to the man's face.

But the bald man was gone.

Instead, a beautiful woman with green eyes, a graceful nose, and full red lips lay where he had been, struggling to get away from Marco. He was caught off guard and loosened his grip, but managed to tighten it again before she got away. "I don't know what you're doing but it's not going to work! Tell me how to let them go!"

The woman pressed her lips together as she tried to pull his hands off her throat. Then, she squeezed her eyes shut and rocked her head from side to side. The tips of the auburn hair slowly darkened to a deep chestnut, the color seeping up toward the roots, and then the long brown hair began to recede, sinking back into her scalp until it was about the same length as Marco's.

Marco gasped and struggled to keep his grip on the brown-haired man that lay there, clutching Marco's arms.

"Stop it!" yelled Marco. "Stop it!" He tightened his grip.

The man's face turned red.

Marco shook his head. "I swear, if you don't tell me how to—"

The man's green eyes bulged as Marco squeezed harder, and after a few more seconds, his lips were a twinge of blue. "Tell me!" Marco squeezed more, until the man's grip on Marco's arms loosened, and his hands slowly slid to the ground, lifeless. His eyes shut as his head lolled to one side.

"Marco!" Sarah screamed.

Instantly, Marco released his grasp and crawled off,

kneeling beside him. He placed one ear on the man's chest.

"Is he still alive?" asked Sarah.

Marco heard a heartbeat. "Yeah." He sat back up and held a hand in front of the man's nose. He felt a slight breath and sighed with relief. "I didn't mean to. I got carried away. I just wanted him to tell me—"

As the man lay there, motionless, the ends of his chestnut hair lightened, the blondness moving up the hair, as the straight strands shortened a bit and began to curl. The man's tan face paled, while freckles popped up on his cheeks and nose, which had changed, and become smaller, younger versions.

A boy lay there.

A thin, blond, freckle-faced boy in a blue jumpsuit.

Marco gasped. His heart pounded as the truth flooded through him.

A boy.

The Curator was a boy.

LOST

BONUS MATERIALS

GOFISH

QUESTIONS FOR THE AUTHOR

S. A. BODEEN

What sparked your imagination for the Shipwreck Island series?

I'm a huge fan of *The Swiss Family Robinson*, and the idea of giving it a bit of a modern reboot appealed to me very much. I did live on a remote island for a couple of years with my family, which helped a little bit.

Who or what most motivated you to complete this novel?

I didn't exactly know what was going to happen in Book 3, so I wanted to finish *Lost* and see where I needed to go next.

Where did you like to write while working on this novel?

I did get to spend some time in Hawaii, pretending to do research while sitting on the beach. I wrote the rest in the winter, some during a snowstorm. . . .

Which character do you think you are most like?

I'm a bit like Sarah. I want to be in charge, but I don't always know what I'm doing.

Who do you most relate to?

I probably relate most to Yvonna, a mom wanting her kids to be safe.

We have to ask . . . if you were shipwrecked on a desert island, who and what would you want with you?
I would want books and snacks. Plenty of each.

Who do you think would win in a fight: a giant coconut crab or a four-winged bird with teeth?
Have you *seen* a coconut crab tear apart a coconut? Google it. The bird, even with teeth, wouldn't stand a chance.

What is your favorite mythical creature?
I love dragons. They terrify me, but I'm drawn to them.

What are some of your favorite shipwreck movies and books?
Some of my favorite books as a child were *Two on an Island* and *Baby Island*. I read them over and over. *Lord of the Flies, Life of Pi*. *Lost* is my favorite television show ever, hands down. I still love to watch *Swiss Family Robinson,* and of course, *Cast Away* and *The Island of Dr. Moreau*. Anything slightly weird on an island, and I'm sold. Plus, I grew up watching *Gilligan's Island* every day after school.

If you could give anybody who's shipwrecked any advice, what would it be?
Do not get shipwrecked on an island that I've created. You will not have any fun and might not get off it alive. . . .

How did you research the Shipwreck Island series?
I needed to bone up on all things sailboat, so I asked a friend who sails to take a look at my story. I had gotten basically everything wrong, so he helped a lot. There were some other things I needed to research, but they apply to Books 3 and 4, and shall remain under wraps for now.

What can we expect from the next book in the series, *Trapped*? (No spoilers, please!)

Trapped picks up right where *Lost* leaves off. We get a few more answers, but then, we also get more questions. . . .

SQUARE FISH

WHAT WILL HAPPEN TO SARAH AND HER FAMILY AFTER THEY MEET

THE CURATOR?

KEEP READING FOR A SNEAK PEEK!

The boy opened his eyes and slowly sat up. He held his palms out toward Marco.

"Please don't. I mean you no harm."

"'No harm'?" Marco's eyes narrowed. "Seriously?"

Sarah pointed toward the closest row of white modules, where her father stood motionless, like a specimen in a test tube. "You . . . you froze my dad!"

"And my brother." Marco pointed down the row.

Sarah glanced at the modules, where Nacho and the dog, Ahab, stood in the same kind of cold stasis as her father. A rush of heat made its way up her insides.

"How could you do that?" she cried. She took in the strange scene around her—all those containers, all those animals. "How could you do that to *them*?"

The boy rubbed his throat for a moment as he noticed the net still stuck to Sarah's leg. He told Marco, "Twist the end and you can remove the net."

Marco stepped a few feet away from the boy, until he was next to Sarah. "And why should I trust you?"

"I don't lie," said the boy.

Sarah scowled. "No, you just take innocent people and animals and turn them into . . . into . . . *Popsicles*!"

"But they aren't hurt," protested the boy.

"Then let them out!" Sarah shouted.

Marco added, "Yeah. Then let them out."

The boy shook his head.

Marco twisted the end of the white tube and pointed it at Sarah's leg.

She gasped. "No, Marco! Wait! You don't know what—"

But before she could do anything, a puff of steam came out of the tube. Her leg tingled, and as she watched and waited with a pounding heart, the netting dissolved.

Sarah exhaled.

A knife that had been tangled in the net dropped to the floor. Marco picked up the blade, folded it, and put it in his pocket.

Sarah rubbed her leg for a moment, then bent

her knee a few times. Convinced that she was truly unharmed, she relaxed and took the hand Marco offered her.

"Okay?" he asked as he pulled her up.

She nodded. "Thanks."

They both glared down at the boy. He darted a few looks their way before lowering his gaze to his feet, which were clad in taupe-colored woven shoes. "I'm not your enemy."

"Then who are you?" asked Marco.

"*What* are you?" asked Sarah.

The boy held out his hand.

Sarah glanced at Marco, then stepped forward and helped the boy up.

"Thank you." He brushed his palms on his blue jumpsuit.

"How did you do that?" asked Sarah. "Change bodies?"

Still looking at his feet, the boy said, "It's a long story."

Marco glanced at the modules. "Are you going to let them out?"

The boy's shoulders slumped. "I . . . can't."

Marco pointed the white tube at the boy. "Then I guess we have time for your story."

Sarah's stomach growled.

Marco rolled his eyes.

"What?" Sarah scowled. "I can't help it."

"You're hungry." The boy's words were quick and pointed, as if he was in a hurry. "I can feed you."

Sarah and Marco exchanged a glance. Cash had told them about the food while she'd been imprisoned. How it had made her fall asleep. Sarah shook her head. "We're not eating your food. Cash told us you drugged her."

The boy sighed. "Yes, I did. But I won't do that to you."

Neither Sarah nor Marco said anything. Sarah was so hungry that she considered believing him. Actually, she was beyond consideration. She was ready to eat whatever he put in front of her.

The boy said, "I'll sample it first. You can see." He seemed eager as he pointed to one side of the cavern. "Please. Let me show you to my cabin."

"Cabin?" asked Sarah. "Like on a ship?"

The boy nodded. Sarah and Marco glanced at each other as the boy led the way. Marco followed close behind, still brandishing the white tube, while Sarah brought up the rear. She stopped to take one more look behind her, at the modules that encased her dad and stepbrother and the dog.

"I'll get you out," she whispered. "I promise." And then she turned to follow Marco, hoping that she'd be able to keep her word.

Marco trod carefully as he followed the boy. He kept the weapon raised; he would be stupid to trust him after what they'd just seen. He didn't believe the boy when he said he couldn't release Nacho and John, as well as Ahab and the other animals. In fact, he found it hard to believe anything the boy said, despite his assurance that he didn't lie.

But Marco suspected that Sarah didn't feel the same way. She was scared—and hungry. They would have to stick together if they were going to free Nacho and John and Ahab.

They left the cavern and continued down a narrow white hallway, the walls and floors made of a shiny, glittery tile like nothing he had ever seen. The air in there smelled much fresher than in the cave. They passed a few doors. Was one of them where Cash had been held? Because the last few moments had proved to Marco that—despite his original feeling to the contrary—the girl they found on the beach had been telling the truth about her ordeal. And this didn't exactly ease Marco's mind.

The boy stopped in front of a door, startling Marco. "You go in," he told the boy. "And don't try anything."

The boy's eyes were sad. "I am not going to try anything." He waved a hand. With a whir, the door slipped open to the side.

"Cool," said Sarah from behind Marco.

Marco locked his gaze on the boy and whispered to Sarah, "He's probably trying to distract us. Help me keep an eye on him."

The boy entered the room.

Sarah followed and whispered back to Marco, "I think you can relax a tad."

But Marco didn't think he should relax, even a little. He took a slow, deliberate step into the room, which was as white as the corridor. Cushioned seats lined the sides, not unlike the seats of the *Moonflight*, and a long table connected to one wall.

The boy walked over to a console and opened something that resembled a microwave. "What are you hungry for?"

Sarah said, "A grilled cheese sandwich."

"Sarah!" said Marco.

She huffed. "What? He asked what I wanted and I told him."

"Like he's gonna have stuff to make grilled cheese." Marco rolled his eyes.

"Cash said he gave her a sandwich." Sarah told the boy, "We met Cashmere, you know. The girl you held here. Did you know that was her name?"

The boy shook his head slightly and shuffled through a stack of shiny discs. He inserted one into the side of the pseudo-microwave and pushed a button. A buzz began and then ended a moment later. The boy opened the door, pulled out a plate, and set it down on the table.

Orange cheese oozed enticingly out from between two perfectly browned pieces of bread. Sarah stuck her tongue out at Marco. "Told you."

The boy slid out a chair for Sarah. She quickly sat down and pulled the plate toward her.

"No." Marco pointed at the boy. "You eat first."

Sarah licked her lips as the boy tore off a chunk of the sandwich, then popped it into his mouth and chewed. He swallowed. "Okay?"

Digging into the sandwich with gusto, Sarah didn't wait for Marco's reply. She spoke with her mouth full. "Ish really good."

Marco's mouth watered as he watched Sarah eat. His empty stomach rumbled. "What else can you make?" he asked.

The boy shrugged. "Whatever you want."

"Cheeseburger. With fries. And ketchup." Marco held his breath.

The boy chose a disc, inserted it, and after a brief buzz, opened the door and pulled out a plate with a steaming cheeseburger and crispy-looking waffle fries, an oblong pool of ketchup off to one side.

Marco's mouth fell open. He sat down before the boy had even set the plate in front of him. Marco took a hefty bite of the cheeseburger and had to shut his eyes as he chewed.

Delicious.

Sarah said, "Don't you want him to try it first?"

Marco's eyes shot open and darted to the boy.

The boy shook his head. "There's nothing in the

food. I promise." He sat down on one of the seats against the wall and watched them eat.

Sarah asked, "What's your name?"

"I'm the Cur—"

"No!" interrupted Marco. "I don't want to hear it. Who are you *really*?"